William Shakespeare's Coriolanus: A Retelling in Prose

David Bruce

Published by David Bruce, 2022.

This is a work of fiction. Similarities to real people, places, or events are entirely coincidental.

WILLIAM SHAKESPEARE'S CORIOLANUS: A RETELLING IN PROSE

First edition. July 23, 2022.

Copyright © 2022 David Bruce.

ISBN: 979-8201145217

Written by David Bruce.

Table of Contents

Dedication

Dedicated to Carl Eugene Bruce and Josephine Saturday Bruce

My father, Carl Eugene Bruce, died on 24 October 2013. He used to work for Ohio Power, and at one time, his job was to shut off the electricity of people who had not paid their bills. He sometimes would find a home with an impoverished mother and some children. Instead of shutting off their electricity, he would tell the mother that she needed to pay her bill or soon her electricity would be shut off. He would write on a form that no one was home when he stopped by because if no one was home he did not have to shut off their electricity.

The best good deed that anyone ever did for my father occurred after a storm that knocked down many power lines. He and other linemen worked long hours and got wet and cold. Their feet were freezing because water got into their boots and soaked their socks. Fortunately, a kind woman gave my father and the other linemen dry socks to wear.

My mother, Josephine Saturday Bruce, died on 14 June 2003. She used to work at a store that sold clothing. One day, an impoverished mother with a baby clothed in rags walked into the store and started shoplifting in an interesting way: The mother took the rags off her baby and dressed the infant in new clothing. My mother knew that this mother could not afford to buy the clothing, but she helped the mother dress her baby and then she watched as the mother walked out of the store without paying.

***

The doing of good deeds is important. As a free person, you can choose to live your life as a good person or as a bad person. To be a good person, do good deeds. To be a bad person, do bad deeds. If you do good deeds, you will become good. If you do bad deeds, you will become bad. To become the person you want to be, act as if you already are that kind of person. Each of us chooses what kind of person we will become. To become a good person, do the things a good person does. To become a bad person, do the things a bad person does. The opportunity to take action to become the kind of person you want to be is yours.

Human beings have free will. According to the Babylonian Niddah 16b, whenever a baby is to be conceived, the Lailah (angel in charge of contraception) takes the drop of semen that will result in the conception and asks God, "Sovereign of the Universe, what is going to be the fate of this drop? Will it develop into a robust or into a weak person? An intelligent or a stupid person? A wealthy or a poor person?" The Lailah asks all these questions, but it does not ask, "Will it develop into a righteous or a wicked person?" The answer to that question lies in the decisions to be freely made by the human being that is the result of the conception.

A Buddhist monk visiting a class wrote this on the chalkboard: "EVERYONE WANTS TO SAVE THE WORLD, BUT NO ONE WANTS TO HELP MOM DO THE DISHES." The students laughed, but the monk then said, "Statistically, it's highly unlikely that any of you will ever have the opportunity to run into a burning orphanage and rescue an infant. But, in the smallest gesture of kindness — a warm smile, holding the door for the person behind you, shoveling the driveway of the elderly person next door — you have committed an act of immeasurable profundity, because to each of us, our life is our universe."

In her book titled *I Have Chosen to Stay and Fight*, comedian Margaret Cho writes, "I believe that we get complimentary snack-size portions of the afterlife, and we all receive them in a different way." For Ms. Cho, many of her snack-size portions of the afterlife come in hip hop music. Other people get different snack-size portions of the afterlife, and we all must be on the lookout for them when they come our way. And perhaps doing good deeds and experiencing good deeds are snack-size portions of the afterlife.

Educate Yourself
Read Like A Wolf Eats
Be Excellent to Each Other
Books Then, Books Now, Books Forever

***

In this retelling, as in all my retellings, I have tried to make the work of literature accessible to modern readers who may lack some of the knowledge about mythology, religion, and history that the literary work's contemporary audience had.

Do you know a language other than English? If you do, I give you permission to translate this book, copyright your translation, publish or self-publish it, and keep all the royalties for yourself. (Do give me credit, of course, for the original retelling.)

I would like to see my retellings of classic literature used in schools, so I give permission to the country of Finland (and all other countries) to give copies of this book to all students forever. I also give permission to the state of Texas (and all other states) to give copies of this book to all students forever. I also give permission to all teachers to give copies of this book to all students forever.

Teachers need not actually teach my retellings. Teachers are welcome to give students copies of my eBooks as background material. For example, if they are teaching Homer's *Iliad* and *Odyssey*, teachers are welcome to give students copies of my *Virgil's* Aeneid: *A Retelling in Prose* and tell students, "Here's another ancient epic you may want to read in your spare time."

CAST OF CHARACTERS

Male Characters

Caius Martius, *later named Coriolanus; Coriolanus means "Conqueror of the City of Corioli."*

Cominius, Titus Lartius, *Roman Generals against the Volscians.*

Menenius Agrippa, *friend to Coriolanus; Menenius is an elderly man who is like a father to Coriolanus.*

Sicinius Velutus, Junius Brutus, *old men who are Tribunes of the people.*

Young Martius, *son to Coriolanus.*

A Roman Herald.

Tullus Aufidius, *General of the Volscians.*

Lieutenant to Aufidius.

Conspirators with Aufidius.

A Roman named Nicanor.

A Volscian named Adrian.

A Citizen of Antium.

Two Volscian Guards.

Female Characters

Volumnia, *mother to Coriolanus.*

Virgilia, *wife to Coriolanus.*

Valeria, *a noble lady of Rome, friend to Volumnia and Virgilia.*

Gentlewoman, *attendant of Virgilia.*

Minor Characters

Roman and Volscian Senators, Patricians, Aediles, Lictors, Soldiers, Citizens, Messengers, Servants to Aufidius, and other Attendants.

Scene

Rome and the Volscian country to the south, with the Volscian towns of Corioli and Antium.

Time

Very early Roman Republic. As a young man, Coriolanus helped depose the last King of Rome: Lucius Tarquinius Superbus (flourished 6th century BCE; died 495 BCE). After being deposed, Tarquin fought a number of battles as he tried unsuccessfully to return to Rome and become King again. Coriolanus fought in the last of those battles. Tarquin is traditionally the seventh and last king of Rome, and some scholars believe him to be a historical figure. His reign is dated from 534 to 509 BCE. Rome at this time is far from being an empire.

Note

The patricians are the aristocracy.

The plebeians are the common people.

CHAPTER 1

— 1.1 —

A gang of mutinous citizens, armed with staves, clubs, and other weapons, stood on a street in Rome. These impoverished citizens were plebeians, or common people; the wealthy citizens of Rome were patricians. The Senators of Rome were patricians.

The first citizen said, "Before we proceed any further, hear me speak."

The other citizens replied, "Speak, speak."

"You are all resolved to die rather than to starve?" the first citizen asked.

"We are resolved," most of the other citizens replied.

"First, you know that Caius Martius is chief enemy to the people," the first citizen said.

"We know it," most of the other citizens replied. "We know it."

"Let us kill him," the first citizen said, "and we'll have grain at our own price. Is it a verdict? Are we agreed that we shall kill Caius Martius?"

"No more talking about it," most of the other citizens replied. "Let it be done. Let's go! Let's go!"

The second citizen said, "One word, good citizens."

The first citizen said, "We are accounted poor — both impoverished and bad — citizens. In contrast, the patricians are accounted good citizens. The food that those in authority feast on to excess on would relieve our hunger. If they would give us just the leftovers, as long as they are wholesome and haven't yet gone bad, we might think that they had relieved us humanely, but they think we are too dear — they think that relieving our hunger would be too expensive. The leanness that afflicts us, the spectacle of our misery, is like an item on a balance sheet that shows their abundant net wealth; our suffering is a gain to them. As long as we don't have enough, the patricians will have more than enough.

"Let us revenge this with our pitchforks before we become as lean as rakes, for the gods know I speak this out of my hunger for bread, not out of thirst for revenge."

The second citizen asked, "Would you proceed especially against Caius Martius?"

The other citizens replied, "Against him first: He's a very dog — a ruthless enemy — to the common people."

"Have you considered what service he has done for his country?" the second citizen asked.

"Yes, very much," the first citizen said, "and we could be happy to give him a good reputation for it, except that he pays himself with being proud."

"Don't speak maliciously," the second citizen requested.

"I say to you that what Martius has done that has made him famous, he did it to that end: He did it in order to become famous. Though soft-hearted men can be content to say he did it for his country, he did it to please his mother and in part because of his pride — and he is proud, even up to the altitude of his virtue."

Roman virtue consisted largely of being valiant. The Romans highly valued courage, and no one denied that Martius was courageous.

"What Martius cannot help in his nature, you account a vice in him," the second citizen said. "You must in no way say he is covetous."

"If I must not say he is covetous, I need not be barren of accusations," the first citizen said. "Martius has enough faults, and more, to tire whoever tries to state them all. If I were to list all his faults, I would grow weary before I had named them all."

Shouts were heard coming from where the Roman Senators had been meeting. Other groups of plebeians were rebelling out of hunger, and the Senators had met to discuss the crisis.

"What shouts are these?" the first citizen asked. "The plebeians on the other side of the city have risen in mutiny. Why are we staying here prating in idle conversation? To the Capitol!"

"Let's go!" the other citizens said.

Menenius Agrippa, one of the patricians in Rome, walked over to the common citizens.

"Wait!" the first citizen said. "Who is coming here?"

"It is worthy Menenius Agrippa," the second citizen said. "He is one who has always loved the people."

"He's one who is honest enough," the first citizen said. "I wish all the rest were honest like him!"

Actually, Menenius could be outspoken in his criticism of the plebeians, but he was willing to talk to them. A patrician didn't have to do much to get the approval of many plebeians.

"What work, my countrymen, is in hand?" Menenius asked. "Where are you going with your cudgels and clubs? What is the matter? Tell me, please."

"Our business is not unknown to the Senate," the first citizen said. "The Senators have had knowledge for a fortnight of what we intend to do, which now we'll show them in deeds. They say poor petitioners have strong breaths; they shall know we have strong arms, too."

The strong breaths meant bad breaths, and also strong language.

"Why, masters, my good friends, my honest neighbors," Menenius said, "will you ruin yourselves?"

"We cannot, sir, because we are ruined already," the first citizen said. "We are starving."

"I tell you, friends, the patricians take most charitable care of you," Menenius said. "As for your needs, your suffering in this famine, you may as well strike at the Heavens with your staves as lift them against the Roman state, whose course will continue on the way it takes, cracking asunder ten thousand curbs of stronger link than can ever appear in your impediment against Rome. The Roman government will continue, no matter how many common citizens mutiny against it. The Roman government is far stronger than you.

"As for the dearth of food, the gods, not the patricians, cause the famine, and bowing your knees in prayer to them, and not using your arms to lift weapons against the Senate, must help.

"Alas, you are carried away by calamity to the point of mutiny against the Senate, where more care is given to you than you know, and you slander the helmsmen who guide the state and who care for you like fathers, when you curse them as enemies."

"Care for us! That is true, indeed!" the first citizen said, sarcastically. "They have never cared for us yet. They allow us to starve, while their storehouses are crammed with grain. They make edicts for usury, to support usurers. They repeal daily any wholesome act of law established against the rich, and they provide more piercing, oppressive statutes daily, to chain up and restrain the poor. If the wars don't eat us up, they will; and there's all the love they bear us."

Menenius replied, "Either you citizens must confess that you yourselves are wondrously malicious, or be accused of folly. I shall tell you a pretty tale. It may be that you have heard it so much that it is stale to you, but since it serves my purpose, I will venture to make it a little staler by telling it to you once more."

"Well, I'll hear it, sir," the first citizen said, "yet you must not think to fob off our degrading misfortune with a tale. But since it pleases you to tell the tale, deliver it."

Menenius said, "There was a time when all the body's members rebelled against the belly, accusing it like this: They said that like a gulf or pit the belly remained in the midst of the body, idle and inactive, always stowing away in cupboards the food, never bearing any labor with the rest of the body's parts, doing nothing while the other parts did such instrumental tasks as seeing and hearing, devising, instructing, walking, feeling, and mutually working together in order to minister to the appetites and desires common to the whole body. The belly answered —"

Menenius paused, and the first citizen asked, "Well, sir, what answer did the belly make?"

"Sir, I shall tell you," Menenius replied.

He twisted his belly fat into a smile, and said, "The belly answered with a kind of smile, which never came from the lungs."

A belly smile that comes from the lungs is a belly laugh.

Menenius repeated, "The belly answered with a kind of smile, which never came from the lungs but just like this — for, you see, I may make the belly smile as well as speak —"

Menenius farted and then said, "— it tauntingly replied to the discontented members, the mutinous parts that envied what the belly possessed.

"The belly's response was exactly as fitting and suitable as the way you malign our Senators because they are not like you."

Should the belly mock the complaining members of the belly? Should the citizens malign the Senators?

If the answer to both questions is no, then the Senators ought not to be mocked because the famine was not caused by them. Also, the belly ought not to mock the other members of the body because in fact those members are starving.

If the answer to both questions is yes, then the Senators ought to be mocked because they are holding back food from the citizens. Also, the belly ought to mock the citizens because that accurately expresses the attitude of the belly — the Senators — toward the other parts of the body — the citizens.

"That is your belly's answer!" the first citizen said. "Why, the head crowns our body like a King, the eye is vigilant, the heart provides counsel, the arm acts as our soldier, the leg acts as our steed, the tongue acts as our trumpeter, and other furnishings and petty helps make up this fabric of our body, and if they —"

"What then?" Menenius interrupted. "By God, this fellow speaks and speaks! What then? What then?"

"— and if they should be restrained by the cormorant — greedy — belly, the belly that is the sink and sewer of the body —"

"Well, what then?" Menenius interrupted.

"The former agents — the parts of the body I just mentioned — if they did complain, what could the belly answer?" the first citizen asked.

"I will tell you," Menenius replied. "If you'll bestow a small part — of what you have little — of your patience awhile, you'll hear the belly's answer."

"You're taking your sweet time telling us," the first citizen complained.

"Note this, good friend," Menenius said. "Your most grave belly was deliberate, and took thought, and was not rash like his accusers, and thus answered: 'It is true, my incorporate, joined-in-one-body friends,' said he, 'that I receive first all the food that you live upon, and that is fitting because I am the storehouse and the workshop of the whole body, but, if you remember, I send it through the rivers of your blood, even to the court of the heart and to the throne of the brain, and, through the channels and various parts of man. The strongest muscles and the smallest and least important veins receive from me that natural competency — sufficient supply — whereby they live. And although all at once, you, my good friends' — this said the belly, listen to me carefully —"

"Yes, sir," the first citizen said. "We are listening carefully."

"The belly said, 'Although all at once you cannot see the big picture and you cannot see what I deliver out to each member, yet I can compile records for an auditor that will show that all of you from me receive the flour — the best part of the food — and leave me only the bran.'

"What do you say to this?"

One answer could have been that the citizens' bellies were lean, and Menenius' belly was not.

The first citizen said, "It was an answer. How do you apply this parable to our situation?"

Menenius replied, "The Senators of Rome are this good belly, and you are the mutinous members. If you examine the Senators' counsels and their cares, and if you digest and understand things rightly that concern the welfare of the common people, you shall find no public benefit that you receive unless it proceeds — comes — from the Senators to you and in no way from yourselves.

"What do you think, you, the big toe of this assembly?"

One answer could have been that the citizens worked and were productive and so provided some things for themselves — and for the patricians.

The first citizen said, "Am I the big toe? Why am I the big toe?"

"Because, being one of the lowest, basest, poorest, of this most 'wise' rebellion, you go foremost, like a big toe.

"You rascal, who are worst in blood to run, lead first to win some advantage."

A rascal is a poor hunting dog. Menenius was insulting the first citizen by calling him a dog that is poorly bred and poor at hunting, but that leads the pack of dogs when there is some reward to be gotten.

Menenius then said to the citizens, "But make ready your stout bats and clubs: Rome and her rats are at the point of battle. One side must suffer pain."

Caius Martius, whom the plebeian citizens had earlier talked about killing, walked over to Menenius and the group of citizens.

Menenius greeted him: "Hail, noble Martius!"

Martius replied, "Thanks."

Then he turned to the plebeians and said, "What's the matter, you dissentious rogues, you who, rubbing the poor itch of your opinion, make yourselves scabs?"

The first citizen said sarcastically, "We always have your good words about us."

Martius replied, "He who will give good words to you will flatter those who are beneath abhorring. What would you have, you curs, who like neither peace nor war? War frightens you, and peace makes you proud and rebellious.

"He who trusts to you, where he ought to find that you are lions, finds that you are hares. Where there are foxes, you are geese."

In this society, one kind of sword was known as a fox.

Martius continued, "You are no surer, no, than is the coal of fire upon the ice, or an icy hailstone in the hot sun. Your virtue is to respect as a worthy man a criminal who is punished; your virtue is also to curse the just man who punished the criminal.

"Whoever deserves greatness deserves your hatred because your desires are the appetite of a sick man who desires most that which would increase his evil illness.

"He who depends upon your favors swims with fins of lead and hews down oaks with flimsy rushes. Hang all of you! Should I trust any of you?

"With every minute you change your mind, and call a man noble who was just now the object of your hatred, and you call a man vile who was just now a hero wearing a garland of honor.

"What's the matter that in several places in the city you cry out against the noble Senators, who, under the gods, keep you in awe, you who otherwise would feed on one another?"

Rather than engage in dialogue with a plebeian, Martius asked Menenius, "What's their seeking? What do they want?"

"They want grain at prices they themselves set," Menenius replied. "They say that the city has large stockpiles of grain."

"Hang them! They say!" Martius said. "They'll sit by the fire, and presume to know what's done in the Capitol; who's likely to rise, who thrives and who declines; side with or against factions; and give out conjectural marriages, making some parties strong and making those parties that stand not in their liking feeble below their cobbled shoes.

"They say there's grain enough! I wish that the nobility would lay aside their pity and let me use my sword. I'll make a quarry of heaps of dead bodies with thousands of these hacked-into-pieces slaves; I'll make a quarry as high as I can throw my lance."

In this society, the word "quarry" was used to refer to a heap of dead animals; for example, a heap of deer that had been killed in a hunt.

Menenius said, "No need, these plebeians are almost thoroughly persuaded not to rebel because although they abundantly lack discretion, the better part of valor, yet they are surpassingly cowardly. But I ask you, what does the other troop of rebelling plebeians have to say?"

"That troop has dissolved, hang them!" Martius said. "They said they were an-hungry."

"An-hungry" was a nonstandard way of saying "hungry." By saying the plebeians used the word "an-hungry," Martius was saying that they were hicks.

Martius continued, "They sighed forth proverbs — that hunger broke stone walls, that dogs must eat, that food was made for mouths, that the gods did not send grain for the rich men only. With these shreds of clichés, they vented their complaints."

In this society, the word "vented" meant "expressed" — and "farted."

Martius continued, "Their complaints were answered, and a petition was granted them, a strange one — to break the heart of generosity, and make bold power look pale."

In this society, the word "generosity," in addition to its usual meaning, referred to the patricians. The Latin word "*generosus*" means "of noble birth."

Martius felt that the patricians had been overly generous in meeting the demands of the plebeians, and the patricians would pay for their generosity. In this society, "to break the heart of generosity" could mean "to crush the nobility." "To break the heart" could mean either "to crush the spirit" or "to take the life."

Martius continued, "They threw their hats into the air as if they wanted to hang them on the horns of the Moon, shouting their emulation."

In this society, "emulation" meant "envy." The plebeians envied — and hated — the patricians, according to Martius.

Menenius asked, "What has been granted to the plebeians?"

"Five Tribunes of their own choice to defend their vulgar wisdoms," Martius replied. "One of the Tribunes they elected is Junius Brutus, another is Sicinius Velutus, and I don't know the others — damn!

"The rabble would have first unroofed the city before it so prevailed with me. The rabble will in time overthrow the patricians' power and bring forth greater reasons that argue in favor of insurrection."

Menenius said, "This is strange."

Menenius, like Martius, was against the plebeians having Tribunes.

Martius ordered the plebeians, "Go, get you home, you fragments!"

In this society, "fragments" were bits and pieces of leftover food.

A messenger arrived; he had been rushing to find Martius.

The plebeians stayed to find out what the messenger wanted.

The messenger asked, "Where's Caius Martius?"

"Here I am. What's the matter?"

"The news is, sir, the enemy Volscians have taken up arms against us."

"I am glad of it," Martius said. "Now we shall have means to vent — get rid of — our musty superfluity."

Literally, "musty superfluity" meant "moldy excess food." Martius used it metaphorically to mean "bad-tempered excess plebeians."

Martius said, "Look, our best elders are coming."

The patricians Cominius, Titus Lartius, and some Senators walked over to them, as did the plebeians Junius Brutus and Sicinius Velutus, two of the newly chosen Tribunes.

The first Senator said, "Martius, what you recently told us is true: The Volscians are up in arms."

Martius said, "They have a leader, Tullus Aufidius, who will put you to it. He is a military leader who will put you to the test. I sin in envying his nobility, and if I were anything but what I am, I would wish that I were only he."

Cominius said, "You have fought against each other."

"If one half of the world fought the other half in a war, and he was on my side, I would revolt and go to the other side — I would fight all my wars only against him. He is a lion that I am proud to hunt."

"Then, worthy Martius," the first Senator said, "fight under the command of Cominius in these wars."

"So you have formerly promised," Cominius said.

"Sir, so I have," Martius replied, "and I will do what I have promised."

He then said, "Titus Lartius, you shall see me once more strike at Tullus Aufidius' face."

Seeing that Titus Lartius was wounded, he said, "Are you stiff and sore from your wound? Will you not fight in this war?"

"Caius Martius," Titus Lartius said, "if I have to, I'll lean upon one crutch and fight with the other before I stay behind and not fight in this war."

"You are a true-bred man!" Martius said.

The first Senator said to Martius, "I request your company at the Capitol, where, I know, our greatest and most powerful friends are waiting for us."

Titus Lartius said to Cominius, "You lead us."

He then said to Martius, "You follow Cominius. We will follow you. It is right and worthy that you have priority before us."

Cominius approved: "Noble Martius!"

The first Senator said to the group of plebeians, "Go from hence to your homes; be gone!"

Martius said, "No, let them follow us. The Volscians have much grain; take these rats thither to gnaw in their granaries."

He said sarcastically to the group of plebeians, "Worshipful mutineers, your valor well puts forth shoots — it is very promising. Please, follow us."

The patricians departed to go to the Capitol. The group of plebeians did not follow them, but stole away to their homes.

Sicinius and Brutus, the two plebeian Tribunes, stayed behind and talked.

"Was any man ever as proud as is this Martius?" Sicinius asked.

"He has no equal."

"When we were chosen Tribunes for the people —"

Brutus interrupted: "Did you notice his sneering lips and eyes?"

"No, but I did notice his taunts."

"Once moved to anger, Martius will not refrain from scoffing at and criticizing the gods," Brutus said.

"He will mock the modest Moon," Sicinius said.

The Moon is modest because the Moon-goddess is Diana, a virgin.

Brutus said, "May the present wars devour him. He is grown too proud to be so valiant. He takes too much pride in his courage, and his pride, taken together with his courage, makes him dangerous to us."

Sicinius said, "Such a nature, tickled and gratified by good success, disdains the shadow that he treads on at noon."

At noon, shadows are underfoot, but during the afternoon, the shadows lengthen.

Sicinius continued, "But I wonder whether his insolence will allow him to endure being given orders by Cominius."

"Fame, at which Martius aims, and whose goddess has already well graced him, cannot be better held nor more attained than by a place below the first," Brutus said, "for what miscarries shall be General Cominius' fault, even though he performs to the utmost of a man. If Cominius fails, people will with giddy censure then cry out, 'Oh, if only Martius had been in charge of the war!'"

Sicinius said, "Besides, if things go well, Martius shall get much of the credit. People have such a good opinion of Martius that they will rob Cominius of the praise that he deserves."

"Yes," Brutus said, "half of all Cominius' honors will go to Martius, even though Martius does not earn them, and all of Cominius' faults in the war shall lead to people giving honor to Martius, even though Martius indeed does not deserve any honor for anything he does."

"Let's go from here, and hear how the orders for war are made, and see in what fashion, more than his self-importance, Martius acts during this present situation," Sicinius said.

Brutus replied, "Let's go."

Tullus Aufidius and some Volscian Senators met in the city of Corioli.

The first Senator said, "So, your opinion is, Aufidius, that the Romans know about our plans and know how we are proceeding."

"Isn't this also your opinion?" Aufidius said. "What plans have ever been thought of in this state that could be brought to bodily act before Rome had the means to circumvent them? The Romans always know what we plan to do.

"Four days have not passed since I received a letter from Rome. Let me read the words. I think I have the letter here; yes, here it is."

He read the letter out loud:

"*They have drafted soldiers for an army, but it is not known whether the army will head east or west. The famine in Rome is great, the people are rebellious, and it is rumored that three people — Cominius; your old enemy Martius, who is in Rome worse hated than you hate him; and Titus Lartius, a very valiant Roman — lead these forces prepared for war to wherever it is bent. Most likely it is headed for you. Consider this information carefully.*"

The Volscian territory lay southeast and southwest of Rome.

The first Senator said, "Our army's in the field. We have never yet doubted Rome was ready to fight us."

"Nor did you think it folly to keep your great plans veiled until when they necessarily must reveal themselves," Aufidius said. "It seems that in the hatching — the planning stages — our plot became visible and known in Rome.

"Because of the discovery by the Romans of our plot, we shall fall short of our aim, which was to capture many towns almost before Rome would know what we were up to."

The second Senator said, "Noble Aufidius, take your commission. Hurry to your bands of warriors. Let us stay here alone to guard Corioli. If the Romans lay siege to us, bring your army here to remove the Romans, but I think you'll find that the Romans will not be prepared for us."

"Oh, don't think that the Romans will not be prepared," Aufidius replied. "I speak from certain knowledge and experience that they will be prepared. What's more, some parcels of their army are in the field already, and they are coming only toward us.

"I now leave your honors. If we — my army and me — and Caius Martius chance to meet, it is sworn between us that we shall continue to strike blows at each other until one of us can do so no more."

The Senators said, "May the gods assist you!"

"And keep your honors safe!" Aufidius said.

"Farewell," the first Senator said.

"Farewell," the second Senator said.

Everyone said, "Farewell."

— 1.3 —

In a room in Martius' house, Volumnia and Virgilia sat on low stools and sewed. Volumnia was Coriolanus' mother, and Virgilia was his wife and the mother of his son.

Volumnia said, "Please, daughter-in-law, sing, or express yourself in a more cheerful way. If my son were my husband, I would more freely rejoice in that absence wherein he won honor than in the sexual embraces in his bed where he would show most love. When he was still only tender-bodied and the only son of my womb, when youth with its beauty drew all eyes his way, when a mother would not allow him to be even an hour out of her sight even if Kings would beg her for an entire day to do so, I, considering how honor would befit such a person, and considering that a person's attractiveness was no better than something picture-like to hang by the wall, if the desire for renown made the person not stir and take action, was pleased to let him seek danger where he was likely to find fame. To a cruel war I sent him; from whence he returned, his brows bound with an oaken wreath as a reward for saving the life of a Roman soldier. I tell you, daughter-in-law, my heart sprang not more in joy at first hearing I had given birth to a boy than when I first saw that he had proven himself to be a man."

Virgilia said, "But what if he had died in the war, madam, what then?"

"Then his good reputation would have become my son," Volumnia replied. "I would have found my child in his good reputation. Hear me profess what I sincerely believe: If I had a dozen sons, each in my love alike and none less dear than your and my good Martius, I had rather had eleven die nobly for their country than one voluptuously indulge himself out of combat."

A gentlewoman entered the room and said to Volumnia, "Madam, the lady Valeria has come to visit you."

Virgilia said to Volumnia, "Please, give me permission to retire and be by myself."

"Indeed, you shall not," Volumnia replied. "I think I hear coming toward us the sound of your husband's drum, I think I see him pluck Aufidius down by the hair. I think I see the Volscians shunning Martius, running away from him as children run away from a bear. I think I see him stamp his feet like this"

— she stamped her feet — "and call like this: 'Come on, you cowards! You were begot in fear, although you were born in Rome.' I think I see him wipe his bloody brow with his mailed, aka armored, hand, and then he goes forth, as if he were a harvestman who has been tasked to mow either all the tops of wheat or all the heads of enemy soldiers, or else lose his wages."

Virgilia said, "His bloody brow! Oh, Jupiter, King of the gods, let there be no blood!"

"Go away, you fool!" Volumnia said. "Blood becomes a man more than gilt becomes his trophy. The breasts of Hecuba, Queen of Troy, when she suckled her son Hector, who was the greatest soldier of Troy in the Trojan War, did not look lovelier than Hector's forehead when it spit blood at the Grecian sword, scorning what had wounded it."

She then said to the gentlewoman, "Tell Valeria that we are fit and ready to bid her welcome."

The gentlewoman exited in order to carry out the order.

Virgilia said, "May the Heavens bless my lord and protect him from the deadly enemy warrior Aufidius!"

Volumnia said, "Martius will beat Aufidius' head below his knee and tread upon his neck."

The gentlewoman returned with Valeria. With them was a male usher.

Valeria said, "My ladies both, good day to you."

"Sweet madam," Volumnia said.

"I am glad to see your ladyship," Virgilia said.

"How are you both?" Valeria asked. "You are obviously housekeepers. You stay at home and do housework."

She asked Virgilia, "What are you sewing here? A fine spot of embroidery, indeed! How is your little son?"

"I thank your ladyship," Virgilia said. "My son is well, good madam."

Volumnia said, "He had rather see the swords, and hear a drum, than look upon his schoolmaster."

"On my word, he is his father's son," Valeria said. "I'll swear, he is a very good-looking boy. Truly, I looked at him for an entire half an hour on Wednesday. He has such a resolute bearing. I saw him run after a colorful butterfly, and when he caught it, he let it go again; and he chased after it again; and he fell down and rolled over and over, and again he chased and caught it, and whether his fall enraged him, or for whatever reason, he clenched his teeth together and tore it. I swear to you that he mammocked it! — he tore the butterfly to pieces!"

Volumnia said, "He had one of his father's moods."

"Indeed, he is a noble child," Valeria said.

Virgilia, the child's mother, said, "Madam, he is a crack — a young rascal."

"Come, lay aside your stitchery," Valeria said. "I must have you play the idle housewife with me this afternoon."

Good Roman wives stayed at home while their husbands were away.

"No, good madam," Virgilia said, "I will not go out of doors."

"Not go out of doors!" Valeria said.

"She shall, she shall," Volumnia said.

"Indeed, no, if you please," Virgilia said. "I'll not go over the threshold until my lord — my husband — returns from the wars."

"Bah, you confine yourself at home most unreasonably," Valeria said. "Come, you must go and visit the good lady who lies in — you must visit the good lady who is soon to give birth."

"I will wish her a speedy recovery for after she gives birth," Virgilia replied, "and I will visit her with my prayers, but I cannot go there physically to visit her."

"Why, I ask you?" Volumnia said.

"It is not to save labor, nor is it that I lack charity," Virgilia replied.

"You want to be another Penelope," Valeria said, "yet, they say, all the yarn she spun in Ulysses' absence only filled Ithaca full of moths."

Penelope was the wife of Ulysses, who spent ten years fighting at Troy, and then, because of misfortunes such as captivity, spent another ten years getting back to his home island of Ithaca. He was away so long that people thought he had died, and young men courted his wife, Penelope, who remained faithful to him. Pressed to marry one of the suitors, she said that she would choose one to marry after she had finished weaving a shroud for Ulysses' father. Each day she wove, and each night she unwound the work she had done. Moths are parasites. Moths ate the yarn, and young suitors ate Ulysses' cattle and drank his wine.

Valeria continued, "Come; I wish the cambric cloth you are embroidering were as sensitive to pain as your finger, so that out of pity you might stop pricking it with your needle. Come, you shall go with us."

"No, good madam, pardon me," Virgilia said. "Indeed, I will not go out of doors."

"In truth, if you go with me I'll tell you excellent news about your husband."

"Oh, good madam, there can't be any news yet. Not enough time has passed."

"Truly, I am not jesting with you," Valeria said. "News from him came last night."

"Indeed, madam?" Virgilia asked.

"I am earnest, it is true. I heard a Senator speaking about it. This is the news: The Volscians have an army in the field; against that enemy army, General Cominius has gone to fight, with one part of our Roman army. Your husband and Titus Lartius are camped before the enemy city of Corioli; they have no doubt that they will prevail and make this a brief war. This is true, on my honor; and so, I ask you, go with us."

"Please excuse me, good madam," Virgilia said. "I will obey you in everything hereafter."

"Let her alone, lady," Volumnia said. "As she is now, she will only make uneasy our mirth, which will be better without her."

"Truly, I think she would make our mirth uneasy," Valeria said.

She said to Virgilia, "Fare you well, then."

She then said to Volumnia, "Come, good sweet lady."

She tried once more to persuade Virgilia to go with them: "Please, Virgilia, turn your solemnity out of doors, and go along with us."

"No, at a word, madam; indeed, I must not," Virgilia said. "I wish you much mirth and enjoyment."

"Well, then, farewell," Valeria said.

— 1.4 —

Martius and Titus Lartius stood in front of the enemy city of Corioli. With them were some Roman Captains and soldiers.

A messenger rode up on horseback to them.

"Yonder comes news," Martius said. "I bet that the two armies — ours and theirs — have met in battle."

"I bet my horse against yours that they have not," Lartius replied.

"Done," Martius said.

"Agreed," Lartius replied.

Martius asked the messenger, "Tell us, has our General met the enemy?"

"They lie within sight of each other," the messenger said, "but they have not spoken — fought — as of now."

"So, the good horse is mine," Lartius said.

"I'll buy him from you," Martius said.

"No, I'll neither sell him nor give him to you, but I will lend him to you for half a hundred years," Lartius said.

He ordered the trumpeter, "Summon the townspeople to a parley."

Martius asked the messenger, "How far off lie these two armies?"

"Within a mile and a half."

"Then we shall hear their alarum — their call to arms — and they will hear ours. Now, Mars, god of war, I pray to you, make us quick in our work, so that we with swords steaming with our enemies' hot blood may march from this city in order to help our friends on the battlefield!"

He ordered the trumpeter, who had stayed quiet until Martius had finished speaking, "Come, blow your blast."

The trumpet sounded, and on the city wall appeared two Senators of Corioli.

Martius asked, "Is Tullus Aufidius within your walls?"

A Senator of Corioli replied, "No, nor is there a man who fears you less than he. How much is the amount that we other men fear you? That's lesser than a little."

In other words, Aufidius feared Martius even lesser than a little.

Drums sounded from the battlefield.

The Coriolian Senator said, "Listen! Our drums are calling forth our youth to fight. We'll break down our walls rather than allow them to impound us like animals. Our gates, which now seem to be securely shut, we have bolted with thin, hollow rushes. They'll open by themselves."

A call to arms sounded.

The Coriolian Senator said, "Listen, you. That call to arms came from far away. That is where Aufidius is. Listen, he is doing notable work among your army, which you have cloven and divided in two."

Martius said, "They are at it! They are fighting!"

"Let their noise be our instructions," Lartius said. "Let the noise call us to arms, too! Ladders, ho!"

Some Volscian soldiers marched out of the city gates.

Martius said, "They don't fear us; instead, they issue out of their city to fight us. Now put your shields before your hearts, and fight with hearts more impervious and better tested than shields.

"Advance, brave Titus. The Volscians disdain us much more than we had imagined, and that makes me sweat with wrath.

"Come on, my fellows. Any man who retreats I'll take for a Volscian, and he shall feel the edge of my sword."

The two sides fought, and the Romans were beaten back to their trenches.

Enraged by his soldiers being beaten back, Martius cursed and said, "May all the contagion of the south light on you, you shames of Rome!"

In this society, people believed that a warm wind from the south carried contagious plague northward.

Martius continued, "You herd of — may boils and plagues plaster you all over, so that your stench may make you abhorred further than you can be seen and one of you be able to infect another although the plague germs must travel against the wind for a mile! You souls of geese that bear the shapes of men, how you have run from slaves whom apes would beat! Infernal Pluto, god of the Underworld! Hell!

"All of you have your wounds in the back, which is suitable for the cowards you are. Your backs are red because of your flight, and your faces are pale because of your fear that makes you shake!

"Mend yourselves and charge home to the hearts of the enemy soldiers, or, by the lightning fires of Heaven, I'll leave the foe in peace and make my wars against you.

"Look to it! Come on! If you'll stand fast and stop fleeing, we'll beat the enemy back and follow them to their wives, just like they followed us to our trenches."

The Romans regrouped, and the trumpets sounded. The Volscians fled, and Martius followed them to the gates of Corioli.

Martius shouted, "So, now the gates are open. Now prove to be good seconds and supporters. It is for the followers — we who chase the fleeing Volscians — that Lady Fortune widens and opens the gates, not for the fliers. Watch me, and do as I do."

Martius went through the gates and into the enemy city.

The first soldier said, "That is foolhardy. I won't do that."

The second soldier said, "Nor will I."

The gates closed, and Martius was shut inside the enemy city, alone.

The first soldier said, "See, they have shut him in."

"He is shut in the cooking pot, I am sure. His goose is cooked," the second Roman soldier said.

Titus Lartius, who had been fighting elsewhere, arrived and asked, "What has become of Martius?"

"He has without a doubt been slain, sir," the second Roman soldier said.

"Following the fliers at their very heels," the first Roman soldier said, "with them he entered their city, and suddenly they clapped their gates shut. He is alone in their city, and he alone must fight all the soldiers in the city."

"Oh, noble fellow!" Lartius said. "He is able to feel fear and pain, which his sword cannot, and yet he is more courageous than his sword, and, even when his sword bends, he stands firm.

"You are lost, Martius. A perfect precious red jewel — a carbuncle — even if it were as big as you are, would not be as rich a jewel. You were a soldier even as Cato the Censor wished for, not fierce and terrible only in the strokes of your sword, but also with your grim looks and the thunder-like percussion of your voice, fear of both of which made your enemies shake, as if the world were feverous and trembled."

Lartius' praise of Martius as being a soldier of the kind that Cato the Censor wished for was remarkable, both because that kind of soldier is remarkable and because Cato the Censor lived over three hundred years in the future.

The reign of the last Roman King — whom Coriolanus fought against — ended in 509 BCE. Cato the Censor lived from 224-149 BCE.

The gates of the city opened, revealing Martius, bleeding and still fighting the enemy soldiers.

"Look, sir," the first Roman soldier said.

"It is Martius!" Lartius said. "Let's rescue him and take him away, or else let's fight beside him."

The Roman soldiers entered the city, fighting.

Some plebeian Roman soldiers held spoils they had looted from Corioli.

A plebeian Roman said about his haul, "I will carry this to Rome."

"And I this," a second plebeian Roman said.

"A murrain on it! I thought this was silver," a third plebeian Roman said.

A murrain is a plague that afflicts cattle.

Martius and Lartius, accompanied by a trumpeter, arrived.

Looking at the plebeian Romans who were looting although Cominius was still fighting outside the city, Martius said, "Look here at these movers and shakers who price their honors at a cracked coin! Cushions, lead spoons, products made of iron valued at a coin of little worth, jackets that hangmen would not take but would instead bury with those who wore them, these base slaves, before the fight is not done, loot and pack up. Down with them!

"Listen, what noise Cominius, the General, is making as he and his troops fight! Let's go to him!

"Over there on the battlefield is the man whom my soul most hates, Aufidius, piercing our Romans, so then, valiant Titus Lartius, take enough numbers of soldiers to hold securely the city while I, with those who have the spirit, hasten to help Cominius."

"Worthy sir, you are bleeding," Lartius said. "Your exertion in battle has been too violent for a second course of fighting."

"Sir, don't praise me," Martius said. "I'm not even warmed up. Fare you well. The blood I drop is rather medicinable than dangerous to me. To Aufidius I will appear like I look now, bloody, and I will fight him."

In this society, physicians treated some patients, such as those suffering from too much choler, by bleeding them. By removing some of the patients' blood, physicians hoped to cure the patients.

Lartius said, "May now the fair goddess, Lady Fortune, fall deeply in love with you, and may her great spells misguide your opponents' swords! Bold gentleman, may prosperity be your servant!"

"May she be your friend no less than those she places highest! May she regard you as one of her best friends!" Martius said. "So, farewell."

"You are the worthiest, Martius!" Lartius said.

Martius exited.

Lartius ordered, "Go, sound your trumpet in the marketplace. Call there all the officers of the town, where they shall learn what I will order them to do. Let's go!"

Near the camp of the Roman General Cominius stood Cominius and several Roman soldiers. They had just finished a strategic retreat from the enemy Volscians.

Cominius said, "Catch your breath, my friends. You have fought well. We have come off the battlefield like Romans. We were neither foolish nor foolhardy while standing up to and opposing the enemy, nor were we cowardly as we retired from the battlefield. Believe me, sirs, we shall be charged again. We will fight again. While we have been fighting, we have heard conveyed by gusts of wind at intervals the charges of our friends against the enemy. You Roman gods, make the outcome of their battle as we wish our own, so that both our Roman armies, with smiling faces in the front lines as we meet each other, may give you thankful sacrifice."

A messenger arrived, and Cominius asked, "What news do you bring?"

The messenger said, "The citizens of Corioli have issued out of the city and met Lartius and Martius in battle. I saw our army driven back to their trenches, and then I went away to carry this news to you."

"Although you speak truth, I think you speak not well. This is bad news," Cominius said. "How long is it since this happened?"

"More than an hour, my lord," the messenger answered.

"They are not even a mile distant," Cominius said. "A short time ago, we heard their drums. How could you in traveling a mile consume an hour, and bring your news so late to me?"

"Volscian spies saw me and chased me, so I was forced to wheel three or four miles out of my way to escape from them, else I would have, sir, brought my report to you half an hour ago."

Seeing someone coming, Cominius said, "Who's yonder? Who's that man who is so bloody that it seems as if he has been skinned? Oh, gods, he has the form and bearing of Martius, and I have at previous times seen him looking like this."

Martius shouted to him, "Have I come too late to fight?"

"The shepherd does not know how the sound of thunder differs from the sound of a small tabor drum more than I know the sound of Martius' tongue from the sound of the tongues of every lesser man."

Martius walked over to him and asked, "Have I come too late to fight?"

Cominius said, "Yes, if you are not covered with the blood of enemy soldiers, but are instead wearing your own blood as if you were wearing a cloak."

Martius said, "Oh, let me hug you in arms as sound as when I wooed, and with a heart as merry as when my bride's and my wedding day was done, and candles burned and showed us the way to our bed!"

Cominius said, "Flower of warriors, how is Titus Lartius?"

"He is a man who is busy making decrees, condemning some to death and some to exile, ransoming this man, pitying that man, and threatening another man. He holds Corioli in the name of Rome as if Corioli were like a fawning greyhound on a leash that can be loosed at will. Lartius commands Corioli, which respects his command; Lartius can treat Corioli as well or as badly as he pleases."

Cominius said, "Where is that slave who told me the warriors of Corioli had beaten you back to your trenches? Where is he? Call him here before me."

"Let him alone," Martius said. "He did inform you of the truth, but as for our 'gentlemen,' aka the common rank and file — a plague on them! Tribunes for them! — the mouse never shunned the cat as they flinched away from rascals worse than they."

"How were you able to prevail over the enemy?" Cominius asked.

"Do I have time enough now to tell you?" Martius asked. "I don't think so. Where is the enemy? Are you lords and masters of the battlefield? If not, why have you ceased to fight until you are victorious?"

"Martius, we have been fighting at a disadvantage and have strategically retired from the battlefield."

"How are their soldiers grouped?" Martius asked. "Do you know on which side they have placed their best and most trusted soldiers?"

"My best guess, Martius," Cominius said, "is that the bands of the best men in the front lines are the Antiates, soldiers from their main city of Antium, and over them Aufidius, their very heart of hope, has the command."

"I ask you," Martius said, "by all the battles in which we have fought, by the blood we have shed together, by the vows we have made to endure as friends, that you directly set me against Aufidius and his Antiates, and that you do not delay now, but instead, filling the air with swords raised high and with arrows and spears, we put ourselves to the test and try our best to defeat the enemy this very hour."

"Though I could wish that you were conducted to a gentle bath and balms applied to your wounds, yet I can never dare to deny you what you ask for," Cominius said. "Take your choice of those soldiers who best can aid your action."

"The soldiers who best can aid my action are those who are the most willing. If any such are here — it would be a sin to believe that they are not — who love this paint, this blood, with which you see that I am smeared, and if any soldiers fear less for their own personal safety than they fear a bad reputation — a reputation for cowardice — and if any think that a brave death outweighs a bad life and that his country is dearer than himself, then that sole soldier or as many who are so minded wave their swords like this" — he waved his sword in the air — "to express his disposition, and follow Martius."

The Roman soldiers all shouted and waved their swords, and they lifted Martius up in their arms and threw their hats in the air.

Exulting, Martius said, "Oh, me alone! Do you regard me as the best soldier? Do you want to make me the point of your sword? If these shows are not just outward appearances, but reveal what you have inside you, which of you is not able to defeat four Volscians? All of you are able to hold your own against the great Aufidius and bear a shield as hard as his. A certain number, although I give thanks to you all, I must select from all of you. The rest shall bear the business in some other fight, as occasion will demand. Let's march. I shall quickly choose the troops I will command; I will choose those men who are best suited to fight the enemy."

"March on, my fellows," Cominius said. "Match this impressive display with your actions in battle, and you shall have a share in all the loot with us."

Titus Lartius had stationed guards inside Corioli, and now he was marching with a Lieutenant, other soldiers, and a scout to the sound of drums and trumpets toward Cominius and Caius Martius.

Lartius ordered the Lieutenant, "Let the gates be guarded. Perform your duties, as I have given them to you. If I send for them, dispatch those centuries — battalions of a hundred soldiers each — to come to our aid. The rest of the soldiers will serve to hold the town for at least a short time. If we lose the battle in the field, we cannot keep the town."

"Don't worry about us, sir," the Lieutenant said.

"Go now, and shut your gates upon us," Lartius ordered.

He then said to his guide, "Come; take us to the Roman camp."

Trumpets sounded on the battlefield as Martius and Aufidius met.

Martius said, "I'll fight with none but you because I hate you worse than I hate a promise-breaker."

"We hate alike," Aufidius said. "In all Africa there is not a serpent I abhor more than your fame and envy."

By "fame and envy," Aufidius meant 1) envied fame, 2) fame that I envy, and 3) fame and malice.

People in this society sometimes used hendiadys (hen·di·a·dys), in which one idea is expressed by two words joined with "and." Other societies often prefer to have one word modify the other. For example, "nice and warm" equals "nicely warm," and "sound and fury" equals "furious sound," and "fame and envy" equals "envied fame."

In this society, one meaning of "envy" was "malice."

Aufidius said, "Find steady footing and prepare to fight."

"Let the first one who flinches die as the other's slave, and may the gods doom him afterward!" Martius said.

"If I flee from you, Martius, cry 'holloa' and hunt me as if I were a hare."

"Within these past three hours, Tullus Aufidius, I fought by myself, alone, within the walls of your Corioli, and I did whatever work I pleased to do. This is not my blood that you see covering my face like a mask. If you want revenge for your soldiers whose blood I have shed, force your strength to reach its highest point."

"Even if you were the Hector who was the whip of your bragged-about ancestors, you would not escape me here," Aufidius replied.

The Trojans' best warrior, Hector, was the whip that scourged the Greek warriors during the Trojan War. After Troy fell to the Greeks, Aeneas and other Trojans journeyed to Italy and became important ancestors of the Romans.

Martius and Aufidius fought, and some Volscians came to Aufidius' aid. Martius fought fiercely and drove them back, and the Volscians carried Aufidius away with them.

Aufidius said to the Volscians who had come to his aid, "Your actions have been meddlesome, and not valiant, and you have shamed me with your damned assistance."

31

Trumpets sounded a retreat. The battle was over, and the Romans had won. Accompanied by Roman soldiers, Cominius talked to Martius, whose left arm was in a sling.

Cominius said to Martius, "If I were to tell you about the work that you did this day, you would not believe your own deeds, but I'll report what you have done where Senators shall mingle tears with smiles; where great patricians shall listen and shudder out of fear, and in the end admire what you have accomplished; where ladies shall be frightened, and, gladly thrilled, hear more; and where the dull Tribunes, who, with the musty, stinking plebeians, hate your honors, shall say this, which is against what is in their hearts, 'We thank the gods our Rome has such a soldier.'

"Yet you came to only a morsel of this feast, having fully dined before. At Corioli you had a feast of fighting, and here you came in only near the end of the meal."

Titus Lartius, with his soldiers, returned after pursuing enemy soldiers.

Lartius said, "General Cominius, Martius here is the steed; we are only the caparison — the cloth spread over the saddle. Had you beheld —"

"Please, now, say no more," Martius said. "My mother, who has a charter — the right — to extol and praise those who share her blood, grieves me when she praises me. I have done as you have done; that is, I have done what I can do. I have been induced to fight for the same reasons as you have been; that is, I have fought for my country.

"That man who has only effected his good will has rivaled my act. Any man who has carried out his resolution to fight well for his country has done what I have done."

"You shall not be the grave of your deserving," Cominius said. You shall not bury the praise that you deserve. Rome must know the value of her own hero. It would be a concealment worse than a theft of your honor, no less than a slander, to hide your accomplishments in battle and to be silent about them. Your vouched-for accomplishments deserve more than the spire and top of praises — such praises as we give to you seem modest in comparison to the praises you deserve. Therefore, I ask you, in token of what you are, and not to reward what you have done — to hear me praise you before our army."

"I have some wounds upon my body," Martius said, "and they smart to hear themselves remembered."

"If your wounds would not be remembered," Cominius said, "they well might fester because of infection from ingratitude, and they well might treat themselves with death rather than getting proper medical attention.

"Of all the horses — we have taken a good number of good horses — and of all the treasure we have acquired on this battlefield and in the city of Corioli, we render to you a tenth. Before the treasure is distributed to the army in common, you shall have your choice of treasure and carry it away."

"I thank you, General," Martius said, "but I cannot make my heart consent to take a bribe to pay my sword. I refuse to take a tenth of the horses and treasure, and I will take only my share of what is distributed to the army in common. I will take only an equal share with those who have beheld the doing of my deeds."

Drums and trumpets sounded, and the soldiers cried, "Martius! Martius!" They also threw their hats and lances in exultation. Cominius and Lartius took off their hats and stood bareheaded to show their respect for Martius.

Martius said, "May these same military instruments, drums and trumpets, which you profane by playing them to honor me, never sound again! When drums and trumpets shall on the battlefield prove themselves to be flatterers, then let all the people in courts and cities be composed entirely of false-faced flatterers! When steel grows as soft as the flattering parasite's silk, let the parasite be given an ovation for his 'deeds' in the wars!

"No more, I say! Because I have not washed my nose that bled, or because I have foiled and defeated some debilitated wretch — deeds that without being noticed were done by many others here — you shout out for me hyperbolic acclamations as if I loved for my small accomplishments to be fed with praises seasoned with lies."

"You are too modest," Cominius said. "You are crueler to your good reputation than you are grateful to us who portray you truly. With your forbearance, if you are incensed against yourself, we will put you, like one who intends to harm himself, in manacles, and then we will reason safely with you.

"Therefore, be it known, as it is known to us, to all the world that Caius Martius wears this war's garland — he has won the most honor in battle. In token of this, my noble steed, which is known to the camp, I give to him, with all his trim equipment; and from this time, for what he did at Corioli, call him, with all the applause and clamor of the host, MARTIUS CAIUS CORIOLANUS! Bear the addition nobly forever!"

The additional name "Coriolanus" meant "conqueror of Corioli."

Usually, the Romans put names in this order: personal name, family name, and addition — Caius Martius Coriolanus. Cominius presumably put the family name Martius first because it derived from the name of Mars, god of war.

The trumpets and drums sounded.

Everyone present shouted, "Martius Caius Coriolanus!"

From now on, and especially after the honor of the additional name was announced in Rome, Martius would be known as Coriolanus.

"I will go and wash," Coriolanus said to Cominius, "and when my face is clean and fair, you shall see whether I blush or not. However it be, I thank you. I mean to sit upon your steed, and at all times to undercrest your good addition to the fairness of my power. I will treat the name 'Coriolanus' as it were an additional mark of honor on my coat of arms, and I will do my best and use all my power to live up to that name."

A heraldic achievement fully displays all the heraldic components that the bearer of a coat of arms is entitled to. The coat of arms appears on the escutcheon, or shield. Above the shield appears the helmet. Above the helmet appears the crest, which is a symbol or device. A crest may be a sculpture of an animal. The motto appears at either the bottom or the top of the heraldic achievement.

An addition is a mark of honor added to a coat of arms. It is also an additional name given to a Roman as a mark of honor. For example, Publius Cornelius Scipio became Publius Cornelius Scipio Africanus after defeating the Carthaginians in North Africa. His name contained these elements: personal name, family name, and addition. His family name consisted of two names: Cornelius Scipio. Scipio indicated a branch of the Cornelii family.

Coriolanus said that he would "undercrest your good addition." He meant that he would protect and defend the additional name that he had been given.

Under the crest are the helmet and the shield, which are defensive armor. The crest itself is ornamental.

Cominius said, "So, let's now go to our tent, where, before we sleep, we will write to Rome about our success.

"You, Titus Lartius, must go back to Corioli. Send to us in Rome the best citizens of Corioli, with whom we may negotiate for their own good and ours."

"I shall, my lord," Lartius said.

Coriolanus said, "The gods begin to mock me. I, who just now refused very Princely gifts, am bound to beg for something from my lord General."

"Take it; it is yours," Cominius said. "What is it?"

"I once stayed here in Corioli at a poor man's house," Coriolanus said. "He treated me kindly. During the battle, he cried out to me. I saw him taken prisoner. But then Aufidius came within my view, and wrath overwhelmed my pity. I request you to give my poor host freedom."

"Well begged!" Cominius said. "Even if he had butchered my son, he would be as free as is the wind. Set him free, Titus Lartius."

Lartius asked Coriolanus, "Martius, what is his name?"

"By Jupiter! I have forgotten it," Coriolanus said. "I am weary; yes, my memory is tired. Have we no wine here?"

"Let's go to our tent," Cominius said. The blood upon your face dries; it is time that your wounds should be looked after. Come."

Did Coriolanus remember the name of his poor host in Corioli later? Was the poor host set free?

There is no indication that these things happened.

Tullus Aufidius, bloody, stood in the camp of the Volscians with some soldiers.

"The town of Corioli has been taken!" he said.

"It will be delivered back on good condition," the first soldier said.

By "on good condition," he meant "on good and favorable terms"; the peace treaty that the Volscians and the Romans would make would be fair.

In his answer, Aufidius used "condition" to mean "state." "Good condition" meant "satisfactory state."

"Condition!" he said. "I wish I were a Roman; for I cannot, being a Volscian, be what I am — I can't continue to live as a defeated Volscian. Condition! What good condition can a treaty find in the defeated party who is at the mercy of the winning party?

"Five times, Martius, I have fought against you, and every time you have beaten me, and you would continue to defeat me every time, I think, if we were to fight each other as often as we eat.

"By all the natural elements, I swear that if I ever again meet Martius beard to beard, he's mine, or I am his. My emulation of him — my desire to surpass him — has not that honor in it that it had. I used to think that I would crush him in an equal fight, true sword to true sword, but now I am willing to potch — stab — at him in whatever way wrath or treachery will give me the opportunity to kill him."

"He's the devil," the first soldier said.

"He's bolder, though not so subtle," Aufidius said. "My valor's poisoned because I suffer stain only by him; he is the only one who surpasses me and hurts my reputation in battle. In order to get back at him, my valor shall betray its own honorable nature.

"I want so much to kill Martius that even if he were asleep or in a sanctuary, even if he were not wearing armor or holding weapons, even if he were in a temple or the Capitol where people are guaranteed their safety, even if he were in a temple while priests are praying or making sacrifices to the gods, even if he were in places and during times when all fury is prohibited, I would ignore all these rotten, decayed-with-age privileges and customs and give in to my hatred of Martius. Wherever I find him, even if it were at my home, with my brother guarding and protecting him, even there, against the laws of hospitality that protect guests, I would wash my fierce hand in the blood of Martius' heart.

"Go to the city and learn how it is guarded and who are the people who must be hostages for Rome."

"Won't you go to the city?" the first soldier asked.

"People are waiting for me at the cypress grove south of the city mills," Aufidius said. "Please bring me word there how the world goes so that in accordance with its pace I may spur on my journey."

"I shall, sir," the first soldier said.

CHAPTER 2

— 2.1 —

In Rome, Menenius was talking with Sicinius and Brutus, two Tribunes of the plebeians.

"The augur tells me we shall have news tonight," Menenius said.

Augurs interpreted omens and forecast the future.

"Good or bad?" Brutus asked.

"Not according to the prayer of the people, for they do not love Martius," Menenius replied.

"Nature teaches beasts to know their friends," Sicinius said.

"Please, tell me whom does the wolf love?" Menenius asked.

"The lamb," Sicinius answered.

"Yes, to devour him," Menenius said, "as the hungry plebeians would love to devour the noble Martius."

"He is indeed a lamb that baas like a bear," Brutus said.

"He's a bear indeed, and he lives like a lamb," Menenius said.

In other words, they disagreed in their evaluations of Martius. Brutus believed that Martius was a bear and not a lamb — Martius was dangerous to the plebeians. Menenius believed that Martius was a dangerous bear on the battlefield but a lamb — at least to the patricians — off it.

Menenius continued, "You two are old men. Tell me one thing that I shall ask you."

Menenius was saying that since the Tribunes were old men, they *ought* to be wise men. He was implying that they were *not* wise men.

"We will, sir," they replied.

"What extreme wickedness makes Martius morally deficient that you two don't have in abundance?" Menenius asked.

Brutus replied, "He's poor in no one fault, but well stocked with all of them. He lacks no fault, for he has them all."

"He especially has pride," Sicinius said.

"And he tops all others in boasting," Brutus said.

"This is strange now," Menenius said. "Do you two know how you are thought of here in the city, I mean by us on the right-hand file? Do you?"

The best soldiers were on the right-hand file. By "us," Menenius meant those whom he considered the best citizens of Rome: the patricians.

Sicinius and Brutus asked, "How are we thought of?"

"Because you talked about pride just now," Menenius said, "I need to ask you whether you will be angry if I tell you."

The two Tribunes replied, "Well, well, sir, well. How are we regarded?"

"Why, it is no great matter," Menenius said, "for a very small pretext will rob you of a great deal of patience. Give your dispositions the reins and let them run freely, and be angry at your pleasures, at least if you take it as pleasurable to you in being so. You blame Martius for being proud?"

"We are not the only ones who do, sir," Brutus replied.

"I know you can do very little alone," Menenius said, "for your helps are many, or else your actions would grow wondrously feeble: your abilities are too much like those of an infant for you two to do much alone. You talk of pride: I wish that you could turn your eyes toward the napes of your necks, so you could look at yourselves and make an interior survey of your good selves! I wish that you could!"

"Suppose that we could see ourselves. What then, sir?" Brutus asked.

"Why, if you could see yourselves, then you would discover a pair of undeserving, proud, violent, testy magistrates, alias fools, as any in Rome."

A wisdom story stated that men carry two bags: one in front, and one in back. In the front bag, men carry knowledge of their neighbors' faults. In the back bag, men carry knowledge of their own faults.

"Menenius, you are well enough known, too," Sicinius said.

Sicinius meant that Menenius' faults were also well known.

"I am known to be a whimsical and moody patrician, and one who loves a cup of hot wine with not a drop of allaying, diluting Tiber River water in it," Menenius said. "I am said to be somewhat imperfect because I tend to favor the complainant, who speaks first, in a case of law. I am said to be hasty and tinder-like — quick-to-anger — upon too trivial a reason. I am said to be one who converses more with the buttock of the night than with the forehead of the morning: I stay up late and get up late. I am said to be a man who utters what I think, and I expend my malice in my breath and words.

"Meeting two such wealsmen as you are — I cannot call you Lycurguses — if the drink you give me touch my palate adversely, I make a crooked face at it. I express in my face what I think."

Wealsmen are public servants who are supposed to be devoted to the weal — the well-being — of the state. "Weal" sounds like "well," and the two Tribunes said "well" frequently.

Lycurgus was a statesman who created the constitution of Sparta in Greece. Lycurgus was given credit for wisdom, something that Menenius felt the two Tribunes lacked.

Menenius continued, "I can't say your 'worships' have reported the matter well, when I find the ass in compound with the major part of your syllables."

He meant that much of what they said was asinine, especially when it came to their opinion of Martius. He may also have been saying that as Tribunes they used many words such as "whereas."

Menenius continued, "And although I must be content to endure those who say you are reverend grave men, yet they lie deadly when they tell you that you have good faces."

Lies may be intrinsically sinful, but not all sins are deadly sins. Menenius was saying that the two Tribunes' faces revealed that they were bad men, and that anyone who looked at their faces and told them that they were good men was committing a deadly sin.

Sins can be venial, or they can be mortal: deadly. A deadly sin leads to damnation. Mortal sins deprive the soul of the grace — mercy — of God. Venial sins are less serious and do not damn the soul.

Menenius continued, "If you see my character as I have described it in this map of my microcosm — my face that reveals my little world — it follows that I am known well enough, too! As you have said, people know my character. Therefore, what harm can your bisson conspectuities — your bleary or almost-blind sight — glean out of this character of mine, if — or since — I am known well enough, too?"

Menenius was saying that one of his well-known faults was a kind of honesty. If he disliked something, it showed on his face. For example, if he disliked wine that someone had given him, his dislike showed on his face. His honesty also appeared in his words. Other people might flatter the two Tribunes by saying that the two Tribunes were good men, and Menenius might be forced to tolerate these people's use of flattery, but Menenius himself would tell — and just now had told — the two Tribunes that they were bad men. So what can the two Tribunes learn by looking at Menenius' honest face — a face that everyone knew revealed what he was thinking? They would learn harm — what Menenius really thought about them.

"Come, sir, come, we know you well enough," Brutus said.

Brutus was trying to get along with Menenius, but Menenius did not want that.

Menenius replied, "You don't know me, yourselves, or anything. You are ambitious for poor knaves' hats and legs. You want them to doff their hats and bend their legs as they show respect to you.

"You wear out a good wholesome forenoon in hearing a case between a woman who sells oranges and a man who sells wine taps, and then you adjourn the case, which concerns three pence, to a second day of hearing.

"When you are hearing a matter between one side and another side, if you happen to become sick with the colic, you make faces like over-expressive actors, you set up the blood-red flag and declare war against all patience, and as you roar for a chamber pot, you dismiss the controversy bleeding the more entangled by your hearing."

The court case was bleeding because it was unfinished and unhealed and because the two Tribunes had made the case worse through their hearings into the case. In addition, whatever was excreted into the chamber pot was mixed with blood.

Menenius continued, "All the peace you make in their cause is calling both the parties knaves. You are a pair of strange ones."

Brutus said, "Come, come, you are well understood to be a much better joker for the dinner table than a necessary statesman in the Capitol."

"Our very priests must become mockers," Menenius said, "if they shall encounter such ridiculous subjects as you are. When you speak best to the purpose, it is not worth the wagging of your beards; and your beards deserve not so honorable a grave as to stuff the pincushion of a person who repairs old clothes, or to be entombed in an ass' pack-saddle.

"Always you must be saying that Martius is proud, but Martius, even regarded at a low estimate of his true worth, is worth all your predecessors since

Deucalion, the Greek Noah, although it is very likely that some of the best of your predecessors were people who inherited their jobs as hangmen."

Being a hereditary hangman was a lowly occupation.

Menenius continued, "Good day to your 'worships.' More conversation with you two would infect my brain, since you are the herdsmen of the beastly plebeians. I will be bold and take my leave of you."

Menenius moved a short distance away, but he saw Volumnia, Virgilia, and Valeria coming toward him.

Menenius said, "How are you now, my as fair as you are noble ladies — the Moon-goddess, if she were Earthly, would be no nobler than you. Where do you follow your eyes so quickly?"

Volumnia replied, "Honorable Menenius, my boy — Martius — is approaching. For the love of Juno, let's go."

Juno was the goddess who was the wife of Jupiter, King of the gods.

"Ha! Martius is coming home!" Menenius said.

"Yes, worthy Menenius," Volumnia said, "and he is coming home with the most prosperous approbation. Everyone is acclaiming his military success."

Menenius threw his hat in the air and said, "Take my hat, Jupiter, and I thank you. Hooray! Martius is coming home!"

Volumnia and Virgilia said, "It is true."

"Look, here's a letter from him," Volumnia said. "The state has received another letter, his wife another one, and, I think, there's one at home for you."

Menenius said, "I will make my house reel with my happiness tonight: a letter for me!"

"Yes, certainly there's a letter for you," Virgilia said. "I saw it."

"A letter for me!" Menenius said. "It gives me another seven years of health, during which time I will curl my lip at the physician. The most sovereign prescription in the medical textbook of Galen is but quackery, and compared to this preservative of a letter bearing good news about Martius, Galen's most sovereign prescription has no more reputation than that of a dose of medicine for a horse. Isn't Martius wounded? He has been accustomed to come home wounded."

"Oh, no, no, no," Virgilia said.

"Oh, he is wounded," Volumnia said. "I thank the gods for it."

"So do I, too, if the wound is not too serious," Menenius said. "As long as he brings a victory home in his pocket, the wounds become him."

Wounds acquired in a victory are better regarded than wounds acquired in a defeat.

"On his brows, Menenius, he comes the third time home with the oak garland," Volumnia said.

Martius was coming home crowned in glory, wearing a garland of honor on his head.

Menenius asked, "Has he disciplined — beaten — Aufidius soundly?"

"Titus Lartius writes that they fought together, but Aufidius got away alive," Volumnia replied.

"And it was time for him to run away, too, I'll warrant him that," Menenius said. "If Aufidius had stayed by Martius, I would not have been so fidiused for all the chests in Corioli, and all the gold that's in them."

Menenius had used the name of Aufidius to create a new word, "fidiused," which meant "treated like Martius would treat Aufidius." Fittingly, the word "fidiused" had decapitated the name of Aufidius.

Menenius asked, "Is the Senate possessed of this information? Has it been informed?"

"Good ladies, let's go," Volumnia said.

She then said to Menenius, "Yes, yes, yes; the Senate has letters from the General, wherein he gives my son the whole credit for the victory of the war. Martius has in his actions in this war outdone his former deeds doubly."

"Truly, there are wondrous things spoken about him," Virgilia said.

"Wondrous things!" Menenius said. "Yes, there are, I promise you, and he truly deserves the wondrous things said about him."

"May the gods grant that all these wondrous things said about him are true!" Virgilia said.

"True!" Volumnia said. "Of course, they are true!"

"True!" Menenius said. "I'll be sworn they are true. Where is he wounded?"

He said to the two Tribunes, who were nearby and listening, "God save your good worships! Martius is coming home, and he has even more cause to be proud than before."

He asked again, "Where is Martius wounded?"

Volumnia replied, "In the shoulder and in the left arm there will be large scars to show the people, when he shall stand for his place — when he shall campaign to be elected Consul. He received seven hurts in his body in the final battle in which the tyrant Tarquinius Superbus was repulsed."

Menenius began counting, "One in the neck, and two in the thigh." He calculated mentally and said, "There's nine wounds that I know of."

Volumnia said, "He had, before this most recent military expedition, twenty-five wounds on his body."

"Now it is twenty-seven wounds," Menenius said. "Every gash was an enemy's grave."

The sounds of Martius' entry into Rome filled the air.

Menenius said, "Listen! The trumpets!"

Volumnia said, "These are the ushers of Martius. Before him Martius carries noise, and behind him he leaves tears. Death, that dark spirit, lies in Martius' muscular arm, which, being advanced, declines, and then men die. Martius' arm, holding a sword, is raised, and then it falls and an enemy soldier dies."

Trumpets sounded. Cominius the General and Titus Lartius appeared. In between them was Martius, the newly named Coriolanus, crowned with an oaken garland. Also present were Captains and soldiers, and a herald.

The herald announced, "Know, Romans, that all alone Martius fought within the gates of Corioli, where he has won, along with fame, a name added to Caius Martius; following these names is this name of honor: Coriolanus."

The herald said to Caius Martius Coriolanus, "Welcome to Rome, renowned Coriolanus!"

Trumpets sounded.

The crowd shouted, "Welcome to Rome, renowned Coriolanus!"

Coriolanus said, "No more of this shouting; it offends my heart. Please, no more."

Cominius said to him, "Look, sir, your mother!"

Coriolanus said to Volumnia, his mother, "You have, I know, prayed to and pleaded with all the gods for my prosperity!"

He knelt before his mother. In this society, it was proper for a child to kneel before his parents to show respect; it would be highly improper for a parent to kneel before a child.

"No, my good soldier, get up," Volumnia said to him. "My gentle Martius, worthy Caius, and newly named because of your deeds in battle — what is your new name? Is it Coriolanus I must call you? But, oh, remember your wife!"

Coriolanus had remembered his wife, who was much less outspoken than his mother.

He gently teased Virgilia, his wife, who was crying from happiness, "My gracious silence, I greet you! Would you have laughed if I had come home in a coffin, you who weep to see me in my triumph? My dear, such weeping eyes as you have, the widows in Corioli wear, and the mothers who now lack sons."

Menenius said, "Now, may the gods crown you!"

Coriolanus replied, "And may they continue to keep you alive."

To Valeria, he said, "Oh, my sweet lady, pardon me for not speaking to you earlier."

"I don't know where to turn," Volumnia said. "Oh, welcome home. And welcome, General, and welcome to all of you."

"A hundred thousand welcomes," Menenius said. "I could weep and I could laugh. I am both light and heavy, both happy and sad. Welcome."

Looking at the two Tribunes, Menenius said, "May a curse gnaw at the very root of the heart of anyone who is not glad to see you three: Coriolanus, Cominius, and Lartius! You are three whom Rome should dote on, yet, by the faith of men, we have some old crabapple trees here at home that will not be grafted to your relish — they will not be altered so that they like you."

He continued, "Yet welcome, warriors. We call a nettle but a nettle, and we call the faults of fools simply folly. We must call things what they are; some things we cannot change."

Cominius said, "That is always true; it is always right."

Coriolanus said, "Menenius is always right — always."

The herald shouted for the crowd to step aside and give the procession room to move forward, "Give way there, and let's go on!"

To Volumnia and Virgilia, Coriolanus said, "Give me your hand, and give me yours. Before I shade my head in our own house, the good patricians must be visited, from whom I have received not only greetings, but along with those greetings new honors."

Volumnia said, "I have lived to see you inherit exactly what I wished for and all the buildings of my fancy; the castles I built in the air have become real.

There's only one thing lacking, which I don't doubt that our Romans will give to you."

Coriolanus knew what she meant: a Consulship. The position of Consul was the highest political position in the Roman Republic.

"Know, good mother," Coriolanus said, "I had rather be the Romans' servant in my own way than sway with them and rule them in their own way."

Cominius said, "Let's go on — to the Capitol!"

Cornets sounded, and everyone left except the two Tribunes: Brutus and Sicinius.

"All tongues speak about Coriolanus, and the people who have bleared eyesight put on spectacles in order to see him," Brutus said. "A prattling nursemaid who has been sent into a rapture lets her baby cry while she chats about Coriolanus. The untidy kitchen wench pins her richest lockram around her dirty neck and clambers up the walls to eye him."

Lockram was an inexpensive Breton linen cloth. The "richest" lockram fabric would not be very rich.

Brutus continued, "Benches in front of shops, frameworks projecting from storefronts, and windows are smothered with people, leaden roofs are filled with people, and the roof ridges are filled with people of all kinds sitting astride the ridges as if they were horses. All these people are alike in wanting to see Coriolanus.

"Seldom-seen flamens — priests devoted to a particular god — press among the popular throngs and puff and breathe hard in order to win a vulgar station: one among the common crowd.

"Also, veiled dames commit the war of white and damask-pink — their complexion — in their nicely made-up cheeks to the wanton spoil of Phoebus' burning kisses. They expose their cheeks to the Sun and risk getting a sunburn — something regarded as unattractive in our society.

"Such a pother and fuss are being made over Coriolanus that it is as if whatsoever god is leading him had slyly crept into his human physical faculties and given him the graceful posture and bearing of that god."

"I am sure that he will quickly be made Consul," Sicinius said.

"Then our political positions as Tribune may as well, during his powerful time as Consul, go and sleep," Brutus said. "While he is Consul, he won't allow us to have any influence."

"He cannot temperately transport his honors from where he should begin and where he should end; instead, he will lose those honors he has won," Sicinius said. "He cannot behave in such a way as a politician must behave in order to be popular and to stay in office."

"In that there's comfort," Brutus said.

Sicinius said, "Don't doubt that the commoners, for whom we stand, will because of their long-standing hostility toward Coriolanus forget for the least cause and reason these new honors of his. That Coriolanus will give them that cause or reason I have little doubt — he will be proud to do it."

"I heard him swear that if he were to run for Consul, he would never appear in the marketplace or wear the threadbare garment of humility," Brutus said.

People running for the political office of Consul customarily wore a toga with no tunic underneath. This both showed humility and also made it easy to display wounds that the candidate had acquired while fighting in battles for Rome.

Brutus continued, "He also swore that he would not show, as the custom is, his wounds to the people — he would not beg for anything from people with stinking breaths."

"That's true," Sicinius said.

"It is what he said; these are his words," Brutus said. "He would prefer to miss out on being Consul rather than to carry his election with anything except the petition of the gentry to him, and the desire of the nobles."

"I can wish for nothing better than for him to continue to hold that intention and to put it into execution."

"It is very likely that he will," Brutus said.

"If that happens, the end result for him will be what we want: a sure destruction," Sicinius said.

"A sure destruction is sure to be the end result, whether for him or for our political authorities. To achieve the end we desire, we must remind the common people that Coriolanus has always hated them. We can tell the common people that Coriolanus always would have made them mules to serve his army, he always would have silenced those who pleaded on their behalf, and he always would have taken away their freedoms. He has always held them, in human action and capacity, to have no more soul or fitness for the world than camels in the war, which receive only their provender for bearing burdens, and only sore blows when they sink under their burdens."

"As you say, if we remind the common people of these things at some time when Coriolanus' soaring insolence shall stir and move and vex the people — which time shall not be wanting, if Coriolanus were to be provoked and incited to act that way, and that's as easy to do as to sic dogs on sheep — that will be his fire to kindle their dry stubble, and their blaze shall darken him forever."

A messenger walked over to them.

Brutus asked, "What's the matter?"

"You have been sent for to go to the Capitol," the messenger said. "It is thought that Martius shall be elected Consul. I have seen the dumb — incapable of speaking — men throng to see him and the blind to hear him speak. Matrons have flung gloves, and ladies and maidens have flung their scarfs and handkerchiefs, upon him as he passed. The nobles have bent their knees as if they were before the statue of Jupiter, King of the gods, and the commoners have made a shower and thunder with their hats and shouts. I never saw anything like this."

Brutus said to Sicinius, "Let's go to the Capitol. We will carry with us ears and eyes that seem appropriate for what is going on at this time, but we will also carry with us hearts for the outcome that we are looking forward to."

That event was the downfall of Coriolanus' Consulship.

"I am with you," Sicinius replied.

Two officers — civil servants — spoke together at the Capital, where the Roman Senators would meet. They were laying down cushions on which the Senators would sit.

The first officer said, "Come, come, they are almost here. How many are running to become Consuls?"

"Three, they say," the second officer said, "but everyone thinks that Coriolanus will be elected."

"He's a brave fellow," the first officer said, "but he's proud with a vengeance, and he is not a friend to the common people. He does not love them — he is not a friend to them."

"Truly, there have been many great men who have flattered the common people, but who never were friends to them, and there are many whom the common people have loved, although the common people don't know why. If the common people love without knowing why, they hate upon no better grounds. Therefore, for Coriolanus neither to care whether they love or hate him manifests the true knowledge he has about their dispositions and inclinations, and owing to his noble carelessness and aristocratic indifference he lets them plainly see it."

"If he did not care whether he had their love or not," the first officer said, "he would have wavered impartially between doing them neither good nor harm, but he seeks their hate with greater devotion than they can render it to him, and he leaves nothing undone that may fully reveal that he is their enemy. Now, to seem to cultivate the malice and displeasure of the people is as bad as that which he dislikes, which is to flatter them in order to get their love."

"Because of his deeds in battle, Coriolanus has deserved worthily of his country," the second officer said, "and his ascent is not by such easy degrees as those who, having been accommodating and courteous to the people, and having uncovered their heads and held their hats in their hands as a mark of respect to the common people, without any further deed to recommend them at all to the common people and win their estimation and good report, but he has so planted his honors in their eyes, and his actions in their hearts, that for their tongues to be silent, and not confess so much, would be a kind of ungrateful and ingrate-ful injury. To report anything other than respect for Coriolanus would be an act of malice, that, being obviously undeserved by Coriolanus, would pluck reproof and rebuke from every ear that heard it."

"Let's speak no more about Coriolanus," the first officer said. "He is a worthy man. Let's move out of the way; they are coming."

Trumpets sounded.

Cominius the Consul arrived with Menenius, Coriolanus, Roman Senators, and others, including the Tribunes Sicinius and Brutus as well as some lictors. Lictors were magistrates' assistants, and they carried fasces, the magistrates' symbols of power. The fasces consisted of rods bound together around an ax; they were a symbol of strength in unity.

Coriolanus stood as the Senators took their places and sat on the cushions.

Menenius said, "Having decided what to do about the Volscians and to send for Titus Lartius, it remains, as the main point of this our after-meeting, to reward and repay the noble service of Coriolanus, who has thus defended and upheld his country; therefore, may it please you, most reverend and grave elders, to request the present Consul, who is also the most recent General in our fortunate and valued successes, to report a little of that worthy work performed by Caius Martius Coriolanus, whom we are met here both to thank and to commemorate with honors appropriate to him."

Coriolanus sat.

"Speak, good Cominius," the first Senator said. "Leave nothing out despite the speech's length, and make us think that Rome is lacking in resources to reward Coriolanus rather than that we are unwilling to stretch our resources so that we can reward him properly."

The first Senator then said to the Tribunes, "Masters of the common people, we request that your ears listen very kindly to what is said here and afterward, we request that you use your friendly influence and mediation with the common people to report and grant what is said and transacted here."

Sicinius replied, "We are convened here to consider a pleasing matter, and we have hearts that are favorably inclined to honor and advance the theme of our assembly."

Brutus added, "And we will sooner be happy to do that if Coriolanus bears in his mind a higher value for the common people than he has hitherto prized them at."

"That's off topic," Menenius said. "That's definitely off-topic. I wish that you had remained silent rather than bring that up. Will it please you to hear Cominius speak?"

"Very willingly," Brutus said, "but yet my cautionary remark is more pertinent than the rebuke you give it."

"Cominius loves your people," Menenius replied, "but don't try to make him their bedfellow."

He then said, "Worthy Cominius, speak."

Coriolanus stood up and attempted to leave so that he would not hear the speech praising him.

Menenius said to him, "No, keep your place. Stay here."

The first Senator said, "Sit, Coriolanus; never be ashamed to hear what you have nobly done."

"I beg your honors' pardon," Coriolanus said. "I would prefer to have my wounds heal again than to hear told how I got them."

Brutus said, "Sir, I hope that my words did not cause you to attempt to leave."

"No, sir," Coriolanus replied. "Yet often, when blows have made me stay, I have fled from words. You did not flatter me, and therefore you did not hurt me, but I love your people as they weigh. I love them according to their worth."

This was dangerous dialogue for someone who did not think the plebeians were worth much and who would run for Consul, and so Menenius said to Coriolanus, "Please now, sit down."

Coriolanus replied, "I would rather have someone scratch my head in the sun when the alarum — the call to battle — were sounding than to idly sit and hear my nothing-much deeds monstrously exaggerated."

Then Coriolanus exited.

Menenius said to the Tribunes, "Masters of the people, how can Coriolanus flatter your multiplying spawn — in which there are a thousand bad ones to one good one — when you see now that he would rather risk all his limbs in warfare to gain honor than to use one of his ears to hear about the honor he gained?"

He then said, "Proceed, Cominius."

Cominius said, "I shall lack the voice needed to speak adequately; the deeds of Coriolanus should not be uttered feebly.

"We Romans believe that valor is the most important virtue, and the virtue that most dignifies the person who has it. If this is true, no one individual in this world can match the man I speak of — Coriolanus.

"When Coriolanus was sixteen years old and the deposed King Tarquin had assembled an army to reestablish himself in Rome, he fought beyond the mark of other warriors. Our then military leader with absolute power temporarily granted to him because of the emergency, whom with all praise I point at" — he pointed to Titus Lartius — "saw Coriolanus fight. He saw when Coriolanus with his Amazonian chin — beardless like the chins of the warrior women known as the Amazons — drove the bristled, bearded lips of the enemy soldiers before him. He stood over and defended an overpowered Roman soldier and in the Consul's view slew three opposing soldiers. He met Tarquin himself and struck him so hard that he fell on his knee. In that day's feats, when Coriolanus might have acted like a woman in the scene and cried and ran away, he proved to be best man on the battlefield, and for his reward his brow was bound with an oaken garland of honor.

"Having entered his manhood on that battlefield, he waxed and grew like a sea, and in the brunt of seventeen battles since that first battle he easily surpassed all other warriors to win the honor of wearing the garland.

"As for this last battle, in front of and in Corioli, let me say that I cannot speak too much in his praise. He stopped the soldiers who were fleeing and by his rare example made the coward soldiers turn terror into entertainment. Just like weeds fall before a vessel under sail in a river, so men obeyed him and fell below his prow. His sword was death's stamp; whenever and wherever his sword marked a man, it took that man's life. From his face to his foot, he was a thing that seemed made of blood, and his every motion was regularly accompanied by the cries of the dying. Alone he entered the mortal — deadly — gate of the city of Corioli, which he painted red with the blood of those who met their unavoidable destiny. Without the aid of other soldiers, he came out of the city, and with a sudden reinforcement of troops he struck Corioli like a malignant planet astrologically inflicting plague on a part of the Earth. Now the city was all his.

"When, by and by, the din of war on the battlefield began to pierce his ready and vigilant sense of hearing, then immediately his spirit, redoubled in strength, re-quickened what in flesh was fatigued, and to the battlefield outside the city he came, where he ran steaming with blood over the lives of men, as if it were a perpetual slaughter, and until we called both battlefield and the city ours, he never stood still to ease his breast and catch his breath with panting."

"What a worthy man!" Menenius said.

The first Senator said, "He surely will measure up to and befit the honors that we confer on him."

"Our spoils of war he kicked at and scorned and rejected," Cominius said, "and he looked upon precious things as if they were the common muck of the world. He covets less than poverty itself would give; he rewards his deeds with the doing of them, and he is content that time well spent is an end in itself. Coriolanus is not a man who fights in order to be rewarded with plunder."

"Coriolanus is very noble," Menenius said. "Let him be called for to appear here."

The first Senator said, "Call Coriolanus."

An officer said, "Here he is."

Coriolanus stepped forward.

Menenius said to him, "The Senators, Coriolanus, are well pleased to make you Consul."

"I owe them always my life and my services," Coriolanus said.

"All that remains for you to be elected Consul is that you speak to the common people," Menenius said.

"I ask you to allow me to overleap and not do that customary action, for I cannot put on the gown of humility, stand without a tunic underneath my gown, and entreat the common people, for the sake of my wounds, to give me their votes. I hope that it may please you to allow me to not do that customary action."

Sicinius said, "Sir, the people must have their votes in the election; neither will they abate one jot of ceremony. The common people want all the customary actions to be performed."

Menenius said to Coriolanus, "Do not challenge the Tribunes or the common people. Please, accommodate the custom and take to yourself, as your predecessors have, your honor with your observance of the formality. You can keep your honor although you observe the custom."

Many patricians were willing to pretend to be friends to the common people in order to get their votes and become Consul, but with no intention of helping the common people after being elected. Coriolanus was unwilling to be hypocritical. He disliked most common people, and he felt that he deserved to be Consul without any votes from the common people, and he did not care who knew it.

"It is a part that I shall blush in acting, and this custom might well be taken from the people," Coriolanus said.

He did not believe that the common people ought to have votes in electing a Consul.

Brutus said to Sicinius, "Did you hear that?"

Coriolanus said, "Must I brag to the common people that thus I acted, and thus I did? Must I show them the no-longer-aching scars of healed wounds that I prefer to hide from them? Must I show them the scars as if I had received the scars only so that I could get their votes!"

"Do not insist on not observing the custom," Menenius said to Coriolanus.

He then said, "We commit to you, Tribunes of the people, our intentions toward the common people, and to our noble Consul we wish all joy and honor."

Menenius wanted the two Tribunes to speak positively to the common people they represented about electing Coriolanus Consul.

The Senators shouted, "To Coriolanus may all joy and honor come!"

Cornets sounded. Everyone except Sicinius and Brutus exited.

Brutus said, "You see how Coriolanus intends to treat the common people."

"May they perceive his intent!" Sicinius said. "He will request their votes from them, as if he were contemptuous that what he requested from them should be theirs to give."

"Come, we'll inform them of our proceedings here," Brutus said. "I know that they are waiting for us at the marketplace."

— 2.3 —

Seven or eight citizens stood talking together in the forum — an open-air plaza and marketplace.

The first citizen said, "Once and for all, if Coriolanus requires and asks for our voices of approval and our votes, we ought not to deny them to him."

"We may, sir, if we will," the second citizen said.

The third citizen said, "We have legal power in ourselves to deny him our votes, but it is a legal power that we have no permission and no moral power to use because if Coriolanus shows us his wounds and tell us his deeds, we need to metaphorically put our tongues into those wounds and speak for them; so, if he tells us about his noble deeds, we must also tell him our noble acceptance and appreciation of them."

The common people had received instructions from the two Tribunes, Sicinius and Brutus, to support Coriolanus. They had also received instructions to talk to Coriolanus in small groups rather than one big group. That way, Coriolanus would have to ask many times for votes rather than ask just once.

The third citizen continued, "Ingratitude is monstrous, and for the multitude to be ungrateful and ingrate-ful would be to make a monster of the multitude. Since we are members of the multitude, we would be making ourselves out to be monstrous members."

The first citizen said, "It won't take much help to make the patricians think less of us than they already do. Remember, when we stood up for ourselves about the grain famine, Coriolanus himself did not refrain from calling us the many-headed multitude."

"We have been called that by many people," the third citizen said. "It's not that some of our heads are brown, some black, some auburn, some bald, but that our minds are so diversely colored, and I truly think that if all our wits were to issue out of one skull, they would fly east, west, north, south, and their agreement about one single route to fly would be to immediately fly to all the points of the compass."

"Do you think so?" the second citizen asked. "Which way do you think my wit would fly?"

"Your wit will not as quickly go out as another man's will," the third citizen said. "Your wit is strongly wedged up in a blockhead, but if it were at liberty, it would surely go southward."

Southward was thought to be a place of illness-causing vapors.

"Why that way?" the second citizen asked.

The third citizen replied, "To lose itself in a fog, where being three parts melted away with rotten dews, the fourth part would return for conscience's sake, to help to get you a wife. You are such a blockhead that you need a wife to take care of you."

"You are never without your jokes," the second citizen said. "It's OK — have your little joke."

"Are you all resolved to give Coriolanus your votes?" the third citizen asked. "But that doesn't matter, for the majority carries the election even if a few people don't give him their vote. I say that if Coriolanus would favor and support the common people, there was never a worthier man."

Coriolanus arrived, wearing the customary clothing used to get votes. With him was Menenius.

The third citizen said, "Here comes Coriolanus, and he is wearing the gown of humility. Closely observe his behavior. We are not to stay all together, but to go to where he is standing, by ones, by twos, and by threes. He's to make his requests to individual citizens. Each of us will receive an individual honor in giving him our own votes with our own tongues: He will thank each of us individually for giving him our vote. Therefore follow me, and I will give you instructions about how you shall go to him."

"We will obey you," the common citizens said.

The common citizens exited.

In the middle of a conversation, Menenius said to Coriolanus, "Oh, sir, you are not right. Don't you know that the worthiest men have done this?"

"What must I say to the common citizens?" Coriolanus asked. "'I beg you, sir'? A plague upon it! I cannot bring my tongue to say such sentences as that or these: 'Look, sir, at my wounds! I got them in my country's service, when a certain number of your brethren roared in fright and ran away from the noise of our own drums rather than stay and fight.' My tongue is not a horse that has been trained to obey. My tongue will not speak at the pace a trainer wants it to speak."

"Oh, me! Oh, the gods!" Menenius said. "You must not speak about that. You must ask the common citizens to think kindly about you."

"Think kindly about me!" Coriolanus said. "Hang them! I wish that they would forget me, like they forget the moral precepts that our clergymen throw away by casting them to the common citizens."

"You'll ruin everything," Menenius said. "I'll leave you now. Please, speak to them, I beg you, in a wholesome manner."

He exited.

By "wholesome," Menenius meant "decent," but Coriolanus pretended that he had meant "clean."

Coriolanus said, "I will ask them to wash their faces and to keep their teeth clean."

Two citizens walked over to him, and Coriolanus said, "So, here comes a brace — a pair — of citizens."

A third citizen then walked over to him.

Coriolanus said to the third citizen, "You know the cause, sir, of my standing here."

The third citizen said, "We do, sir; tell us what has brought you to it."

"My own desert."

Coriolanus believed that he deserved to be Consul.

"Your own desert?"

"Yes, but not my own desire."

"Why not your own desire?" the third citizen asked.

"Sir, it was never my desire to trouble the poor with begging," Coriolanus replied.

"You must know that if we give you anything, we hope to gain something from you," the third citizen said.

"Well, then, please tell me your price for the Consulship," Coriolanus said.

The first citizen replied, "The price is to ask for it kindly."

The word "kindly" meant "courteously," and also "with a recognition of kinship between you and us plebeians."

"Kindly!" Coriolanus said. "Sir, I ask you to let me have it. I have wounds to show you, which you shall be permitted to see in private."

He then said to the second citizen, "I want your good vote, sir; what do you say?"

"You shall have it, worthy sir," the second citizen said.

"It's a deal, sir," Coriolanus said. "There's in all two worthy votes I have begged. I have your alms. Adieu."

Now that he had their votes, he wanted no more to do with them.

The third citizen said, "This is somewhat odd."

The second citizen said, "If we had our votes back again — but it doesn't matter."

The citizens might have withheld their votes from Coriolanus if they had them back again, or they might have made him grovel a little or a lot more.

The three citizens exited, and two new citizens arrived.

Coriolanus said to them, "Please tell me now, if it may agree with the tune of your voices that I may become Consul. I have here the customary gown."

"You have deserved nobly of your country," the fourth citizen said, "and you have not deserved nobly."

"What is the answer to your riddle?" Coriolanus asked.

"You have been a scourge to her enemies, and you have been a rod to her friends," the fourth citizen said. "You have not indeed loved the common people."

"You should judge me as being all the more virtuous because I have not been common in my love," Coriolanus said. "I will, sir, flatter my sworn brother, the people, as if they were my comrades-in-arms, in order to earn a dearer estimation of myself from them; it is a form of behavior they account gentle and noble, and since the wisdom of their choice is rather to have my hat than my heart, I will practice the insinuating nod and take off my hat to them most hypocritically and counterfeitly; that is, sir, I will counterfeit the bewitchment of some popular man and give it bountifully to the desirers. Therefore, I ask you to vote for me so I may become Consul."

Coriolanus was wrong about the common citizens. They wanted a friend in high office, not just someone who would treat them politely during the campaign and then ignore them after being elected to high office.

The fifth citizen said, "We hope to find that you are our friend, and therefore we give you our votes heartily."

"You have received many wounds for your country," the fourth citizen said.

"I will not authenticate your knowledge by showing them to you," Coriolanus said. "I will make much of your votes for they are important to me, and so I will trouble you no further."

Both citizens said, "May the gods give you joy, sir, heartily!"

The two citizens exited.

"Very sweet votes!" Coriolanus said sarcastically, disliking having to ask the common citizens for their votes, which he wanted given to him without his having to ask for them. "Better it is to die, better it is to starve, than to beg for the reward that already we have deserved. Why should I stand here in this woolvish — like a wolf wearing sheep's wool — toga, to beg their needless votes from every Tom, Dick, and Harry who appears? The Senators want me to be Consul, and that should be an end to the election — I should not need the votes of the plebeians! But custom calls for me to be here and to wear this woolen toga and to beg for votes. If we should do in all things whatever custom calls for, then the dust on ancient traditions would lie unswept, and mountainous error would be too highly heaped up for truth to see over it."

To some extent, Coriolanus was correct. If Rome always followed ancient tradition, then it would still have a King. But by tradition the patricians had always had the power in Rome, and the plebeians felt that that ought not to be the case.

Coriolanus said to himself, "Rather than to fool it here in the forum like I am, let the high office and the honor go to a man who would willingly do this. But I am halfway through. I have endured the first half, and so the second half I will do."

Three more citizens walked over to him.

Coriolanus said to himself, "Here come more votes."

He said loudly, "I want your votes. For your votes I have fought; I have stayed up at night and guarded you in return for your votes. For your votes I bear two dozen or so wounds. I have seen the sights and heard the sounds of thirty-six battles. For your votes I have done many things, some less, some more. I want your votes. Indeed, I want to be Consul."

The sixth citizen said, "Coriolanus has acted nobly, and he must not go without any honest man's vote."

"Therefore, let him be Consul," the seventh citizen said. "May the gods give him joy, and make him a good friend to the common people!"

The citizens said, "Amen, amen. May God save you, noble Consul!"

They exited.

"Worthy votes!" Coriolanus said.

Menenius arrived, accompanied by Sicinius and Brutus.

Menenius said to Coriolanus, "You have stood in the forum for your allotted time, and the Tribunes endow you with the people's voices of approval and votes. It remains that, wearing the official regalia, you at once meet the Senators."

"Is this done?" Coriolanus asked.

Sicinius replied, "You have discharged the custom of requesting votes. The people admit you to the office of Consul, and you are summoned to meet the Senators at once to ratify your election."

"Where?" Coriolanus asked. "At the Senate House?"

"Yes, there, Coriolanus," Sicinius replied.

"May I change these garments?"

"You may, sir," Sicinius replied.

"That I'll do immediately; and, knowing myself again, I will go to the Senate House," Coriolanus said.

"I'll keep you company," Menenius said to Coriolanus.

He then asked the two Tribunes, "Will you go along with us?"

"We will stay here and meet the common people," Brutus replied.

Sicinius said, "Fare you well."

Coriolanus and Menenius exited.

Sicinius said to Brutus, "He has the Consulship now, and by his looks I think it is dear to his heart."

"Coriolanus wore his humble clothing with a proud heart," Brutus said. "Will you dismiss the common people?"

Some citizens walked over to the two Tribunes.

"Hello, my masters!" Sicinius said. "Have you chosen to vote for Coriolanus?"

"He has our votes, sir," the first citizen said.

"We pray to the gods that he may deserve your love and respect," Brutus said.

"Amen, sir," the second citizen said. "To my poor unworthy notice, he mocked us when he begged for our votes."

"Certainly he jeered at us downright," the third citizen said.

"No, it is his way of speaking," the first citizen said. "He did not mock us."

The second citizen said, "There is no one among us, except yourself, who doesn't say that Coriolanus used us scornfully. He should have showed us his marks of merit, his wounds that he received for his country."

"Why, so he did, I am sure," Sicinius said.

"No, no," the citizens replied. "No man saw them."

"He said he had wounds," the third citizen said, "which he could show in private; and with his hat, thus waving it in scorn, 'I want to be Consul,' says he. 'Ancient custom, except by your votes, will not so permit me; give me your votes therefore.' When we granted him our votes, he said, 'I thank you for your votes — your most sweet votes. Now that you have left your votes with me, I have no further use for you.' Was not this mockery?"

Sicinius asked, "Were you too ignorant to see it, or seeing it, were you of such childish friendliness that you gave your votes to him?"

Brutus asked, "Couldn't you have told Coriolanus — as you were instructed to say — that when he had no power, but was only a petty servant to the state, he was your enemy and always spoke against your liberties and the rights that you bear in the body of the commonwealth, and now, arriving to a position of power and state authority, if he should still malignantly remain a steadfast foe to you the plebeians, your votes might be curses to yourselves?

"You should have said that as his worthy deeds claim no less than what he stood for, so his gracious nature ought to have consideration for you in return for your votes and his gracious nature ought to transform his malice towards you into love and respect, speaking out for you as your patron."

Sicinius said, "If you had said this, as you were previously advised to say, you would have tested his spirit and found out which way he was inclined — for you or against you. From him you would have plucked his gracious promise, which you might, as occasions had warranted, have held him to. Or else what you said would have galled his surly, arrogant nature, which does not easily endure any conditions tying him to anything. By so putting him in a rage, you would have been able to take advantage of his anger and passed by him, leaving him unelected."

Brutus said, "Did you perceive that he solicited you in frank and open contempt when he needed your love and respect, and do you think that his contempt shall not be bruising to you, when he has power to crush you? Why didn't your bodies have any heart among you? Or did you have tongues that cried out against the rule of reason and good sense?"

"Have you before now denied your votes to the asker?" Sicinius said. "And now again you have bestowed your voices of approval and votes — which candidates are supposed to plead for — to a person who did not ask for them, but instead mocked you."

"Coriolanus has not been confirmed as Consul," the third citizen said. "We may still deny him office."

"And we will deny him office," the second citizen said. "I'll get five hundred voices to protest against him taking office."

The first citizen said, "I will get twice five hundred citizens and their friends to add to your five hundred."

Brutus said, "Go immediately, and tell those friends that they have chosen a Consul who will take from them their liberties and rights. This Consul will make them of no more voices — or votes — than dogs that are as often beaten for barking as they are kept to do that barking."

Brutus was saying that Coriolanus would expect the citizens to "bark" at the enemy during wartime, but if the citizens "barked" for civil rights, the new Consul would have them beaten.

"Let the citizens assemble," Sicinius said, "and on a sounder judgment let all of them revoke your simple-minded election of Coriolanus as Consul. Emphasize Coriolanus' pride, and his old hatred for you plebeians; in addition, don't forget with what contempt he wore the humble suit of clothing and how in his suit of clothing he scorned you. But the respect you have for him, as you thought upon his services he had rendered to Rome, took away from you the apprehension of his present and proud carriage, which very sarcastically and without the gravitas a Consul needs, he fashioned after the inveterate hate he bears you. You respected him so much because of his military prowess that you did not see at first his haughty bearing that disqualifies him to be a Consul."

Brutus said, "Lay the fault on us, your Tribunes; say that we urged that no obstruction should cause you not to support him, but that you must cast your votes for him."

Sicinius said, "Say that you chose him more because we commanded you to than because you were guided by your own true emotions, and say that your minds, preoccupied with what you must do rather than with what you should do, made you go against the grain of your own desires to vote him in as Consul: Lay the fault on us."

"Yes, don't spare us," Brutus said. "Say that we lectured to you. We told you how young he was when he began to serve his country, how long he continued to serve his country, and what stock he springs from — the noble family of Martius, from which family came Ancus Martius, Numa's daughter's son, who, after great Hostilius, here in Rome was King. From the same noble family came Publius and Quintus, who had conduits constructed that brought our best water here. And the nobly named Censorinus, who was twice chosen Censor by the people, was his great ancestor."

Numa Pompilius was King of Rome from 715-673 B.C.E., Tullus Hostilius was King of Rome from 673-642 B.C.E., and Ancus Martius was King of Rome from 642-617 B.C.E. They were Rome's second, third, and fourth Kings.

Brutus and Sicinius knew that some of the people they had mentioned as being among Coriolanus' ancestors would worry the citizens. Some of his ancestors were Kings, and the common people would worry that Coriolanus, who was aristocratic and proud and who looked down upon the plebeians, would want to be King.

The job of a Censor in Rome was to keep the official list of all the citizens; the Censor also supervised public morals. Running afoul of the Censor would cause major problems for any plebeian unlucky enough to be in that position.

Brutus, however, wanted to protect his and Sicinius' butts. Despite bringing up things that they knew would worry the plebeians against Coriolanus and his ancestors, they did mention one good thing that two people Coriolanus was related to had done: the construction of the aqueducts to bring water to Rome.

A Consul can be a friend to the plebeians and do good things for them, but Coriolanus was not a friend to the plebeians.

Sicinius said, "One thus descended, who has in addition worked hard in his own right to achieve high office, we Tribunes commended to your remembrances and asked you to vote for, but you have found, metaphorically weighing in a set of scales his present proud bearing with his past, that he's your fixed enemy, and therefore you revoke your sudden and hasty approbation."

Brutus said, "Say that you would never have elected Coriolanus as Consul — harp continually on that — except because of us Tribunes urging you to vote for him. Quickly, when you have gathered a good number of your fellow citizens who regret Coriolanus' election, go to the Capitol."

"We will do so," the citizens said. "Almost all repent the way they voted in this election."

The citizens exited.

Brutus said, "Let them go on. It is better to risk this mutiny than to wait for a greater mutiny — and a greater risk — that would, no doubt, occur later.

"If, as Coriolanus' nature is, he falls into a rage with their refusal to give him their votes, we will both observe and take advantage of his anger."

"Let's go to the Capitol," Sicinius said. "We will be there before the stream of the common people, and this mutiny shall seem, as partly it is, their own, although we have goaded them on to rebel."

Brutus and Sicinius had done a good job of covering their butts. The citizens would make clear to the patricians that the two Tribunes had urged them to vote for Coriolanus.

CHAPTER 3

— 3.1 —

On a street in Rome walked Coriolanus, dressed as a Consul. With him were Menenius, many patricians, Cominius, Titus Lartius, and many other Senators. They were walking to the forum.

Coriolanus said, "So Tullus Aufidius has raised a new army?"

"He has, my lord," Lartius said, "and it was that which caused our coming to terms swifter than we had expected to."

"So then the Volscians stand as they did at first, before the most recent battle, ready, when time and occasion shall prompt them, to make inroads and raids upon Rome again," Coriolanus said.

"They are worn out and exhausted, lord Consul," Cominius said, "and so it is hardly likely that in our lifetimes we shall see their battle banners wave again."

"Did you see Aufidius?" Coriolanus asked.

"On a guarantee of safe conduct, he came to me," Lartius said, "and he cursed the Volscians because he said that they had so vilely yielded the town of Corioli to us. He has retired to Antium, the capital city of the Volscians."

"Did he speak about me?" Coriolanus asked.

"He did, my lord," Lartius said.

"What did he say?" Coriolanus asked.

"He spoke about how often he had met you in battle, sword to sword. He said that of all things upon the Earth he hated you the most. He said that he would pawn his fortunes and possessions with no hope of ever recovering them provided that he might be called your vanquisher."

"And he is living at Antium?" Coriolanus asked.

"Yes, at Antium," Lartius replied.

"I wish I had a reason to seek him there, so I could oppose his hatred fully," Coriolanus said.

He then said to Lartius, "Welcome home."

The two Tribunes, Sicinius and Brutus, walked toward them.

Seeing them, Coriolanus said, "Look, these are the Tribunes of the people. They are the tongues of the common mouth; they are the advocates of the common people. I despise them because they dress themselves in authority, against all noble endurance. We patricians find them disgusting."

"Go no further," Sicinius said.

"What are you saying?" Coriolanus asked.

"It will be dangerous for you to go on," Brutus said, "Go no further."

"What is the reason for this change?" Coriolanus asked.

"What is the matter?" Menenius asked.

"Hasn't Coriolanus been approved by both the nobles and the common people?" Cominius asked.

"Cominius, he has not," Brutus said.

Coriolanus knew that the nobles had approved of his being elected Consul, so the common people must have changed their minds and votes, like children would. He asked, "Have I had children's voices of approval and their votes?"

"Tribunes, give way," the first Senator said. "Coriolanus shall go to the marketplace."

"The people are incensed against him," Brutus said.

"Stop," Sicinius said, "or all will fall into turmoil."

"Are these your herding animals?" Coriolanus asked the two Tribunes. "Must these common people have votes, these common people who can give their votes and immediately take them back again? What are your offices? What are your duties? Since you are their mouths, why can't you rule their teeth? Have you not set them on against me?"

Coriolanus was comparing the common people to animals. First, he compared them to a herd, and then he compared them to dogs that had been set on against a man — they had been ordered to attack a man the way that dogs attacked bears in bear-baitings.

"Be calm, be calm," Menenius advised him.

"This is a planned, premeditated thing, and it grows by plot. Its purpose is to curb the will of the nobility. If we suffer it, we will live with people who cannot rule and will not ever be ruled."

"Don't call it a plot," Brutus said. "The people cry that you mocked them, and recently, when grain was given them gratis, you complained; you scorned the suppliants for the people, and you called them time-servers, flatterers, foes to nobleness."

"Why, this was known before the election," Coriolanus said.

"Not to them all," Brutus said.

"Have you informed them since then?" Coriolanus asked.

"What!" Brutus said, pretending to be shocked by such a question. "I inform them!"

"You are likely to do such business," Coriolanus said.

"I am not unlikely, in every way, to do your business better than you do," Brutus said.

"Why then should I be Consul?" Coriolanus said. "By yonder clouds, let me deserve so ill as you, and make me your fellow Tribune."

Sicinius said to Coriolanus, "You show too much of that characteristic about which the people rise in revolt. If you will pass to where you are bound — the marketplace and the Consulship — you must inquire your way, which you are out of, with a gentler, more courteous spirit, or never be so noble as a Consul, nor join and cooperate with Brutus as a Tribune. To become Consul, you must treat the common people much better."

"Let's be calm," Menenius advised.

"The common people have been deceived and misled," Cominius said. "Proceed. This petty bickering is not suitable for Rome, nor has Coriolanus deserved this so dishonorable obstacle that has been laid treacherously in the plain way of his merit. Coriolanus deserves to be Consul."

"You tell me about grain!" Coriolanus said to Brutus. "This was my speech, this is what I said, and I will speak it again —"

"Not now, not now," Menenius said.

"Not in this heat, sir, now," the first Senator said.

A hot day can make tempers rise, and so can a hot argument.

"Now, as I live, I will speak it again," Coriolanus said. "As for my nobler friends, I beg their pardons. As for the mutable, rank-scented many, let them know that I do not flatter, and therefore they can use me to behold themselves. For them, I am a mirror, and I will let them know what they really are. I say again, in soothing and flattering the common people, we nourish against our Senate the cockle — the weeds — of rebellion, insolence, sedition, which we ourselves have plowed, sowed, and scattered, by mingling them with us, the honored number, who do not lack virtue, no, nor power, except that which they — the patricians — have given to beggars."

"Say no more," Menenius said.

"Say no more words, we beg you," the first Senator said.

"What! No more!" Coriolanus said. "I have shed my blood for my country, not fearing outward force, and so my lungs shall coin words until their decay against these scabs, these common people, which we disdain should afflict us, yet we patricians as a group sought the precise way to catch them."

"You speak of the common people as if you were a god able to punish them, and as if you were not a man of their infirmity," Brutus said. "You speak as if you were a god, not a mortal."

"It would be well that we let the people know it," Sicinius said.

"Know what?" Menenius asked. "Coriolanus' words spoken in anger?"

"Anger!" Coriolanus said. "Even if I were as patient as the midnight sleep, by Jove, everything I said would still be what I think in my mind!"

"It is a mind that shall remain a poison where it is, and not poison any further," Sicinius said.

He meant that Coriolanus would not be allowed to become Consul, and therefore would not have the influence that would allow him to spread what the two Tribunes considered to be the poison of his mind. Sicinius spoke as if he had the power to ensure that that happened.

"Shall remain!" Coriolanus said. "Do you hear this Triton of the minnows? Do you hear this big shot of the little people? Do you hear his absolute 'shall'?"

Triton is a minor sea-god.

The absolute "shall" was Sicinius saying — or at least implying — that Coriolanus absolutely shall not be allowed to become Consul.

Cominius said, "What Sicinius said goes beyond the power of the Tribunes. He was out of order."

Coriolanus said, "'Shall'! Oh, good but very unwise patricians! Why, you grave but reckless Senators, have you thus allowed the many-headed monster Hydra — the plebeians — here to choose an officer, who with his peremptory 'shall,' being but the monster's noisy horn, does not lack the spirit to say he'll turn your current in a ditch, and make your channel his? He intends to use your power and your resources for his own purposes. If he has power, then bow down to him in your ignorance; if he has no power, then awaken and snap out of your dangerous lenity to the common people. If you are wise, then don't be like common fools; if you are not wise, let the plebeians have cushions and sit by you as fellow Senators.

"You are plebeians, if they are Senators — and they are no less than Senators, when, with the voices of the plebeians and the patricians blended together, the greatest taste most palates theirs. The taste of the legislation passed will be most pleasing to the plebeians; in other words, you will see that the plebeians have more power than the patricians. The plebeians choose their magistrate, this Tribune, and he is such a one as puts his 'shall,' his popular 'shall' of the plebeians against a graver bench — the Senate — than ever frowned in Greece. By Jove himself, it makes the Consuls base and of lower rank, and my soul aches to know, when two authorities are roused up, and neither is supreme, how soon destruction and chaos may enter between the gap of both and use the one to destroy the other."

Cominius said, "Well, let's go on to the marketplace."

Coriolanus said, "Whoever gave that advice to give the plebeians the grain of the storehouse gratis, as it used to happen sometimes in Greece —"

Menenius said, "Well, well, no more of that."

"— though there in Greece the people had more absolute power," Coriolanus said, "I say that they nourished disobedience and fed the ruin of the state."

"Why, shall the people give one who speaks like this their vote?" Brutus said. "Should the common people vote for someone like Coriolanus?"

"I'll give my reasons for my belief, reasons that are much worthier than their votes," Coriolanus said. "They know the grain was not our recompense to them for good service rendered. They are well assured that they never did service for the grain. After being drafted into the war, even when the navel — the vital center — of the state was threatened, they would not thread — go through — the gates and fight. This kind of 'service' did not deserve grain gratis. During the war, their mutinies and revolts, wherein they showed the most valor — certainly more valor than they showed in actual battles against the enemy — did not speak well for them. The accusation that they have often made against the Senate, that the patricians hoarded grain, has no basis in fact, and this accusation could never be the motive of our so generous donation. Well, what then? How shall this monster of many stomachs digest and understand the Senate's courtesy? Let deeds express what's likely to be their words: 'We requested the grain, we plebeians outnumber the patricians, and because the patricians truly feared us, they gave us what we demanded.' Thus we debase the nature of our seats and make the rabble call our cares fears, and this will in time break open the locks of the Senate and bring in the crows to peck the eagles."

"Come, that's enough," Menenius said.

"It's more than enough, with over-measure," Brutus said.

"No, take more," Coriolanus said. "What may be sworn by, both divine and human, seal and confirm what I end with! This double worship, this divided authority of patrician and plebeian, where with reason the patricians disdain the plebeians, where without any reason the plebeians insult the patricians, where gentry, title, wisdom, cannot reach an agreement except by the yea and nay of the ignorance of common people — this divided authority of patrician and plebeian must neglect real necessities, and give way the while to unstable trivialities.

"When planning is barred like this, it follows that nothing is done according to plan. Therefore, I beg you — you who wish to be less fearful than discerning, you who love the constitution of the government more than you fear a violent change that is necessary to preserve it, you who prefer a noble life to a long life, and you who wish to risk curing a sick body with a dangerous medicine when the body is sure to die without it — I beg you to at once pluck out the multitudinous tongue and deprive the common people of a say in the government. Don't let the common people lick the sweet that is their poison. Your dishonor in granting power to the plebeians mangles true judgment and bereaves the state of that integrity and unity that should become and dignify it because since the plebeians have power, the Senate does not have the power to do the good it would do for the evil common people who now control it."

Brutus said, "Coriolanus has now said enough."

"He has spoken like a traitor, and he shall be held accountable for it as traitors are," Sicinius said.

"You wretch, may despite overwhelm you!" Coriolanus said. "What should the common people do with these bald — devoid of hair and of intelligence — Tribunes? The common people lean and depend on the Tribunes, and they fail in their obedience to the greater bench — the Senate. In a rebellion, when what is not right but could not be avoided became law, the Tribunes were elected. In a better hour, let it be said that what was the right thing to do was in fact done, and now let us throw the Tribunes' power in the dust."

"This is manifest treason!" Brutus shouted.

"Make this man a Consul!" Sicinius said. "No!"

"Aediles, come here!" Brutus shouted.

Aediles could make arrests.

An Aedile appeared.

Brutus pointed at Coriolanus and said, "That man needs to be arrested!"

Knowing that one Aedile could not accomplish that task, Sicinius ordered him, "Go, call the common people."

Sicinius then said to Coriolanus, "In the name of the common people, I myself arrest you because you are a traitorous rebel, an enemy to the public commonwealth. Obey me, I order you, and follow me to your trial."

"Get away from me, you old goat!" Coriolanus said.

The Senators said, "We'll be the surety for him. We'll guarantee that he shows up in court."

"Aged sir, keep your hands off him," Cominius said.

"Get away from me, you rotten thing," Coriolanus said, "or I shall shake your bones out of your garments!"

"Help, citizens!" Sicinius shouted.

A rabble of plebeian citizens arrived with the Aediles.

"On both sides we need more respect," Menenius said.

Sicinius pointed to Coriolanus and said to the Aediles and the common people, "Here's the man who would take from you all your power."

"Seize him, Aediles!" Brutus ordered.

"Down with him! Down with him!" the plebeians shouted.

The Senators shouted, "We need weapons! Weapons! We need weapons!"

All was a mass of confusion, with everyone shouting.

"Tribunes!"

"Patricians!"

"Citizens!"

"What!'"

"Sicinius!"

"Brutus!"

"Coriolanus!"

"Citizens!'"

'Peace! Peace! Peace!"

"Stay! Wait! Peace!"

"What is going to happen?" Menenius said. "I am out of breath; ruin and destruction are near; I cannot speak. You Tribunes, talk to the people! Coriolanus, be calm! Speak, good Sicinius."

"Hear me, people," Sicinius shouted. "Peace!"

"Let's hear our Tribune," the plebeians shouted. "Peace! Speak! Speak! Speak!"

"You are on the point of losing your liberties," Sicinius said to the plebeians. "Martius would take them all from you — Martius, whom recently you have voted for Consul."

This was not what Menenius had wanted Sicinius to say.

Menenius said, "Damn! Damn! Damn! This is the way to kindle a fire, not to quench one."

The first Senator said, "This is the way to unbuild the city and to lay all flat."

"What is the city but the people?" Sicinius asked.

"True," the plebeians shouted. "The people are the city."

"By the consent of all," Brutus said, "we were established the people's magistrates. We were elected Tribunes."

"You so remain," the plebeians said.

"And so you are likely to remain," Menenius said.

"That is the way to lay the city flat," Coriolanus said. "That is the way to bring the roof to the foundation, and take that which is still orderly laid out and turn it into heaps and piles of ruin."

"This talk deserves death," Sicinius said.

"Either let us maintain and uphold our authority, or let us lose it," Brutus said. "We do here pronounce, upon the part of the common people, by whose power we were elected to wield power on their behalf, that Martius deserves immediate death."

Brutus did not refer to Martius by his honorable new name: Coriolanus.

"Therefore lay hold of him," Sicinius ordered the Aediles. "Carry him to the Tarpeian rock, and from that cliff throw him down to his destruction."

"Aediles, seize him!" Brutus ordered.

"Surrender, Martius, surrender!" the plebeians shouted.

"Listen to me speak one word," Menenius said. "I beg you, Tribunes, hear me speak a single word."

"Quiet! Quiet!" the Aediles shouted.

Menenius said to Brutus, "Be that which you seem to be, truly your country's friend, and temperately proceed to what you would thus violently redress."

Brutus replied, "Sir, those cold ways, which seem like prudent helps, are very poisonous where the disease is violent."

Brutus ordered the Aediles, "Lay hands upon him, and carry him to the rock."

"No, I'll die here," Coriolanus said. He drew his sword and said, "Some among you have seen me fight. Come, try upon yourselves what you have seen me do to others. Fight me if you dare."

"Down with that sword!" Menenius said to Coriolanus.

Menenius then said, "Tribunes, withdraw for awhile."

Brutus ordered, "Lay hands upon him."

Cominius shouted, "Help Martius! Help him, all of you who are noble! Help him, young and old!"

"Down with him! Down with him!" the plebeians shouted.

The two sides fought, and the Tribunes, Aediles, and plebeians were beaten back. They retreated.

Menenius said to Coriolanus, "Go, get you to your house! Be gone! Leave! All will be lost and ruined, if you don't leave!"

"Get you gone," the second Senator said.

"Stand fast," Cominius said. "Let's make a stand. We have as many friends as enemies."

"Shall it come to that?" Menenius asked.

"May the gods forbid!" the first Senator said. "Please, noble friend, Coriolanus, go home to your house; leave it to us to cure this disease."

"Because this is a sore upon us," Menenius said, "you cannot treat yourself. Leave, I beg you."

Cominius said to Coriolanus, "Come, sir, come along with us."

Coriolanus said about the plebeians, "I wish that they were barbarians — as they are, although they were littered in Rome. I wish that they were not Romans — as they are not, although they were calved in the porch of the Capitol building —"

"Leave," Menenius said. "Don't express your worthy rage with your tongue. One time will owe another — another time will come that will make up for this time."

Coriolanus said, "On fair ground I could beat forty of them."

Cominius said, "I myself could take on a brace — a pair — of the best of them. Yes, I myself could take on the two Tribunes. But now the odds are against us — they are beyond calculation, and manhood is called foolery when it stands against a falling building. Will you leave from here before the ragtag crowd returns? Their rage rends like obstructed waters that flow over the banks that normally hold them in."

"Please, be gone," Menenius said to Coriolanus. "I'll try whether my old intelligent, good judgment is in fashion with those who have but little. This quarrel must be patched with cloth of any color. I need to find a way — any way that works — to talk us out of this mess."

"Let's leave," Cominius said to Coriolanus.

Coriolanus and Cominius exited.

The first patrician said, "This man, Coriolanus, has marred his fortune."

"His nature is too noble for the world," Menenius said. "He would not flatter Neptune even if it would get him possession of Neptune's trident, and he would not flatter Jove even if it got him Jove's power to thunder."

Neptune was the god of the sea; a symbol of his power was his trident — his three-pronged spear.

Jove was Jupiter, King of the gods. His weapon of choice was the thunderbolt.

Menenius continued, "His heart's his mouth. He expresses in words whatever he feels and holds nothing back."

A proverb of the time stated, "What the heart thinks the tongue expresses."

According to Ecclesiasticus 21:26, "*The heart of fools is in their mouth: but the mouth of the wise is in their heart*" (King James Version).

Menenius continued, "Whatever his breast forges, that is what his tongue must vent and express. And, when he is angry, he forgets that he ever heard the name of death."

He heard some noises; the plebeians were returning.

He said, "Here's goodly work!"

The second patrician said, "I wish they were in bed!"

"I wish they were in the Tiber River!" Menenius said. "What the Hell! Why couldn't Coriolanus speak civilly to them?"

Brutus and Sicinius returned, along with the rabble of plebeian citizens.

Sicinius said, referring to Coriolanus, "Where is this viper who would depopulate the city and be every man himself?"

"You worthy Tribunes —" Menenius began.

Sicinius interrupted, "He shall be thrown down from the Tarpeian rock with rigorous, pitiless hands. He has resisted the law, and therefore the law shall scorn him by denying him any trial other than the severity of the public power that he so sets at naught."

The first citizen said, "He shall well know that the noble Tribunes are the people's mouths, and we the people are the Tribunes' hands."

The citizens said, "He shall, that's certain."

"Sir, sir —" Menenius began.

"Be quiet!" Sicinius ordered.

Menenius said, "Do not cry havoc, where you should hunt only with modest warrant."

To cry havoc is to give the command to kill indiscriminately, not sparing the rich nobles. Menenius was saying that the Tribunes did not have the authority to cry havoc; their authority was much less.

Sicinius said, "Sir, how comes it that you have helped to make this rescue?"

He was using "rescue" in a legal sense — Menenius had helped Coriolanus to escape the legal authorities who had arrested him. Of course, force had been used in this escape.

"Hear me speak," Menenius said. "I know the Consul's worthiness, and I can also name his faults —"

"Consul!" Sicinius said. "What Consul?"

"The Consul Coriolanus," Menenius replied.

"He a Consul!" Brutus said.

"No! No! No! No! No!" the citizens shouted.

"If, with the Tribunes' permission, and yours, good people, I may be heard, I would like to say a word or two," Menenius said. "Listening a moment to me shall cause you no further harm than a little loss of time."

"Speak briefly then," Sicinius said, "for we are determined to execute this viperous traitor."

People in this society believed that vipers were born by eating their way out of their mother's body. Vipers were symbols of treachery.

Sicinius continued, "To banish him from Rome would be but one danger, and to keep him here in Rome would mean our certain death; therefore, it is decreed that he dies tonight."

The "one danger" of banishment that Sicinius was thinking of was a bad relationship between Coriolanus' family and the plebeians.

Menenius said, "Now may the good gods forbid that our renowned Rome, whose gratitude towards her deserving children is enrolled in Jove's own book, should now, like an unnatural dam, eat up her own!"

A dam is an animal mother.

"He's a disease that must be cut away," Sicinius said.

"Oh, he's a limb that has only a disease," Menenius said. "It would be mortal to cut it off and amputate it; to cure it is easy. What has he done to Rome that deserves death? He has killed our enemies, and he has lost blood — the blood he has lost, I dare to say, is more by many an ounce than the blood that he has in his body now — he dropped his blood for his country. And if he were to lose what blood he has left because his country took it from him, then all of us — all who do it and all who allow it to be done — would bear a brand, a mark of infamy, until the end of the world."

Genesis 4:15 states about Cain, who murdered Abel, his brother, "*And the LORD said unto him [Cain], Therefore whosoever slayeth Cain, vengeance shall be taken on him sevenfold. And the LORD set a mark upon Cain, lest any finding him should kill him*" (King James Version).

The sign for Cain was a mark of infamy, although it protected him. Exodus 20:13 states, "*Thou shalt not kill*" (King James Version). Modern translations often state, "*You shall not murder*." Murder is morally wrong, and although Cain had sinned by murdering Abel, God did not want the violence to be perpetuated, and so God protected Cain's life.

Sicinius said, "What you said is clean *kam*. It is completely crooked."

"*Kam*" is a Welsh word for "crooked."

Brutus said, "It is completely awry. When he loved his country, it honored him."

Menenius said, "The service of the foot, after it has become infected with gangrene, is not at that time respected for what it was before it was infected."

"We'll listen no more to you," Brutus said. "Pursue him to his house, and pluck him out of it, lest his infection, being of a catching nature, spreads further."

"One word more, one word," Menenius said. "This tiger-footed rage, when it shall find the harm of unthinking swiftness, will too late tie leaden weights to its heels. Swift rage, unaccompanied by thought, leads to bad consequences. Proceed by the process of law, lest factions break out — because Coriolanus is beloved by many — and Romans sack great Rome."

Brutus began, "If that were true —"

"What are you saying?" Sicinius said. "Have we not had a taste of Martius' 'obedience'? Our Aediles smote? Ourselves resisted? Come on!"

"Consider this," Menenius said. "He has been bred in the wars ever since he could draw a sword, and he is ill schooled in refined language; he throws good flour and bad bran — good words and bad words — together without distinction. Give me permission, and I'll go to him, and undertake to bring him to where he shall peacefully answer the charges against him in a lawful courtroom, even if the outcome means the utmost peril to him — even if the outcome is being sentenced to death."

"Noble Tribunes," the first Senator said, "it is the humane way: The other course of action will prove too bloody, and the end of it is unknown to the beginning. You don't know how it will end."

"Noble Menenius," Sicinius said, "you then act as the people's officer. You bring Martius to the court to stand trial."

Sicinius then ordered, "Masters, lay down your weapons."

Brutus said to Sicinius, "Don't go home. This needs to be done quickly."

Sicinius said to Menenius, "Meet us in the marketplace. We'll wait for you there, where, if you don't bring Martius, we'll proceed in our first way: We will find him and execute him."

"I'll bring him to you," Menenius replied.

He said to the Senators, "Let me ask for your company. Coriolanus must come to the marketplace, or the worst will follow."

The first Senator said, "Please, let's go to him."

Coriolanus talked with other patricians in a room of his house.

Coriolanus said, "Let them pull all Rome down about my ears, give me death on the wheel or at wild horses' heels, or pile ten hills on the Tarpeian rock, so that the precipice stretches down beyond the range of sight, yet I will always be like this to them. I will continue to act as I always have."

He was unwilling to change even if it meant that Rome must lie in ruins or that he would be executed either by being tied to a wheel and being beaten to death or by having his limbs tied to four horses that then rode away in different directions.

"You do the nobler act by doing this," a patrician said. "It is better to act like the patrician you are than to bow down to the plebeians."

Coriolanus said, "I wonder that my mother does not approve more of my actions, for she has been accustomed to call the plebeians woolen vassals — poor people who wear coarse clothing made of wool. She also called the plebeians things created to buy and sell with coins of little value, to show bare heads in assemblies after taking off their hats to show respect to their betters, to yawn, to be still and to wonder, when one of my rank stood up to speak about peace or war."

While he was talking, his mother, Volumnia, entered the room.

Seeing her, Coriolanus said, "I am talking about you. Why did you wish me to be milder when talking to the plebeians' Tribunes? Would you have me be false to my nature? You should rather say that I should play the man I am. It is better for you to advise me to be myself."

"Oh, sir, sir, sir," Volumnia said. "I wish that you had put your power well on, before you had worn it out," metaphorically comparing the Consulship to clothing.

She continued, "It would have been better for you to have officially been declared Consul before you began to act like yourself. Now your Consulship is gone."

"Let it go," Coriolanus said.

"You might have been enough the man you are, with striving less to be so," Volumnia said. "You could have been the man you are without showing so openly your contempt for the two Tribunes. Lesser had been the thwartings of your purposes and inclinations, if you had not shown the plebeians how you were disposed before they lacked the power to cross and thwart you. If you had been officially declared Consul, the two Tribunes would not have been able to stop you from being yourself."

"Let them hang," Coriolanus said.

"Yes, and burn, too," Volumnia said.

Menenius and some Senators entered the room.

"Come, come," Menenius said to Coriolanus. "You have been too rough, somewhat too rough. You must return and mend things."

"There's no remedy," the first Senator said. "You must do that, for if you don't, our good city will be cloven in the middle, divide into hostile factions, and perish."

"Please," Volumnia said to Coriolanus, "listen to him. I have a heart as little yielding and submissive as yours, but I have still a brain that leads my use of anger to better advantage. My brain lets me know the right time to show my anger."

"Well said, noble woman," Menenius said. "Before he should thus stoop to the herd, except that the violent feverous seizure of the time craves it as medicine for the whole state, I would put on my armor, which because of my old age I can scarcely wear. But because of the times we live in, he must do what he does not want to do."

"What must I do?" Coriolanus asked.

"Return to the Tribunes," Menenius replied.

"Well, what then?" Coriolanus asked. "What then?"

"Repent what you have spoken," Menenius replied.

"Repent for them!" Coriolanus said. "I cannot do it for the gods, so must I then do it for the plebeians?"

"You are too uncompromising," Volumnia said, "though therein you can never be too noble, except when crises declare themselves. I have heard you say that honor and craftiness, like inseparable friends, grow together in wartime. Grant that, and then tell me what each of them loses by the other that makes it impossible for the two to be inseparable friends in peacetime."

"Bah! Bah!" Coriolanus said.

"On the contrary, she asked a good question," Menenius said.

"If it is honorable in your wars to be deceitful in order to achieve your most important goals, how is it less or worse to use deceitfulness in peacetime since the use of deceit is necessary both in war and in peace?" Volumnia asked.

"Why are you urging this?" Coriolanus asked. "Why are you urging me to be deceitful?"

"Because now it is incumbent on you to speak to the common people," Volumnia said. "You must not say what your own feelings make you want to say, and you must not say those things that your heart prompts you to say; instead, you must use such words that are only learned by rote in your tongue, although such words are only bastard syllables that have nothing whatsoever to do with what you are truly thinking.

"Now, this use of deceit no more dishonors you at all than to capture a town with gentle words, a town whose capture otherwise would make you trust to the fortune of war and to hazard much blood.

"I would be deceitful and appear to be what I am not if my honor required the use of deceit to protect my fortunes and my friends. In saying this, I am the representative of your wife, your son, these Senators, and the nobles. But you prefer to show the louts of Rome how you can frown than to spend a fawning look and a fawning word upon them so that you can get their friendship and safeguard that which the lack of their friendship might ruin. You prefer to frown at the plebeians rather than to act civilly to them so that you get their support and safeguard both your life and your Consulship."

"Noble lady!" Menenius said. "Come, go with us; speak civilly to the Tribunes. You may heal not only what is dangerous now, but also the loss of what is past. You may not only protect Coriolanus' life now, but also get back for him his Consulship."

Volumnia acted out what she wanted her son to do as she described the actions: "I beg you now, my son, go to them, with this hat in your hand, and thus far having held it out ... play along with them ... with your knee kissing the stones ... for in such business action is eloquence, gestures speak more persuasively than words, and the eyes of the ignorant are more learned than their ears ... nodding your head and often bowing in all directions, thus correcting your proud heart, and making it as humble as the ripest mulberry that will not endure the handling."

Mulberries are so soft when ripe that they are crushed when they are picked. Because of this, they became a symbol for submissiveness.

Volumnia continued, "Then say to them that you are their soldier, and because you were bred in broils and raised in wars, you do not have the soft way of acting that, you confess, it would be suitable for you to use — just as they claim — when you ask them for their good friendship, but you will adapt yourself, truly, and be hereafter their friend, so far as you have power and person."

"If you do this, just as she said," Menenius said, "why, the plebeians' hearts would be yours, for they give pardons as freely as they speak words to little purpose."

"Please," Volumnia said, "go now, and be ruled by my advice, although I know you would rather follow your enemy into a fiery gulf than flatter him in a ladies' chamber."

She looked up and said, "Here comes Cominius."

Cominius walked over to them and said, "I have been in the marketplace; and, sir, it is fitting that you get yourself a strong party of armed supporters, or that you defend yourself by calmness of words and actions, or that you defend yourself by absence. You need bodyguards, you need to placate the plebeians with your words and actions, or you need to keep away from the marketplace. Everything is in upheaval; all the plebeians are angry."

"Only fair speech will work," Menenius said. "Coriolanus must speak civilly to the plebeians."

"I think that will work, if Coriolanus can restrain his spirit enough to do that," Cominius said.

"He must, and he will," Volumnia said.

She said to Coriolanus, "Please, say now that you will, and then go and do it."

"Must I go show the plebeians my unbarbed sconce — my uncovered head?" Coriolanus asked. "Must I take off my hat and show them respect? Must I with base tongue give my noble heart a lie that it must bear? Well, I will do it. Yet, if there were but only this body to lose — this body that will fill a single plot of earth when I die, this clay that is Martius, the plebeians should grind it to dust and throw it against the wind."

Something that Coriolanus valued more than his life was at stake: the approval of his mother.

Coriolanus continued, "Go to the marketplace! You have now given me such a part to play that I can never perform convincingly."

"Come, come, we'll prompt you," Cominius said.

Volumnia said, "Please, sweet son, you have said that my praises made you first a soldier, so in order to have my praise for this, perform a part you have not played before. Do this for me."

"Well, I must do it," Coriolanus said. "Go away, my natural temperament, and let some harlot's spirit possess me! Let my throat of war, which harmonized with my drum, be turned into a piping voice as small in volume and as high in pitch as that of a eunuch or the virgin voice that lulls babies asleep! Let the smiles of knaves camp in my cheeks, and let schoolboys' tears obstruct my eyes! Let a beggar's tongue make motion through my lips, and let my armed knees, which bowed and bent only while in my stirrups, bend like the knees of a beggar who has received an alms!"

As he spoke, he grew angrier and angrier, and now he said, "I will *not* do it, lest I cease to honor my own truth and by my body's action teach my mind a most irremovable and base degradation."

"Do as you choose, then," Volumnia said. "For me, your parent, to beg for anything from you is more to my dishonor than it would be for you to beg for anything from the plebeians.

"Let all go to ruin. Let your mother rather feel your pride than fear your dangerous obstinacy, for I mock at death with as big a heart as yours. Do as you wish. Your valiantness comes from me, for you sucked it from my breasts, but your excessive pride comes from yourself."

"Please, be calm," Coriolanus said. "Mother, I am going to the marketplace. Chide me no more. I'll mountebank their loves, I'll climb on a platform and lie and cheat their hearts from them, and I will come home beloved by all the tradesmen in Rome. Look, I am going. Give my kind regards to my wife. I'll return as Consul, or never again trust what my tongue can do in the way of flattery."

"Do as you will," Volumnia said.

She exited.

"Let's go!" Cominius said. "The Tribunes are waiting for you. Prepare yourself to answer them mildly, for they are prepared with accusations that I hear are stronger than those already charged against you."

"The word is 'mildly,'" Coriolanus said. "Please, let's go. Let them invent accusations against me. I will answer in accordance with my honor."

"Yes, but also mildly," Menenius said.

"Well, mildly let be it then," Coriolanus replied. "Mildly!"

Sicinius and Brutus spoke together in the marketplace.

Brutus said, "We will attack him with all the force we can on this point: Coriolanus seeks tyrannical power. If he evades us there, we will emphasize his malice toward the common people, and that the plunder gotten when he invaded the territory of the Antiates was never distributed among the soldiers."

An Aedile walked over to them.

Brutus asked the Aedile, "Will Coriolanus come?"

"He's coming," the Aedile replied.

"Who is accompanying him?" Brutus asked.

"Old Menenius, and those Senators who have always favored him."

Sicinius asked the Aedile, "Do you have a catalogue of all the votes that we have procured set down by majority vote?"

The two Tribunes were rigging things in the plebeians' favor. There were two ways of voting. Voting by tribes involved majority rule. Each tribe would vote according to what the majority in that tribe wanted. Since the plebeians outnumbered the patricians, this method of voting favored the plebeians. Another method of voting gave more weight to wealthy voters than impoverished voters and so favored the patricians.

"I have it," the Aedile replied. "It is ready."

"Have you collected the voters by tribes?" Sicinius asked.

"I have," the Aedile replied.

"Bring the people here to the marketplace immediately," Sicinius said, "and when they hear me say, 'It shall be so in the right and strength of the common people,' whether it be for death, for fine, or for banishment, then if I say 'Fine' let them cry 'Fine,' and if I say 'Death' let them cry 'Death.' The common people must insist on their long-established rights and prerogatives and on the exercise of power in the truth of their cause."

"I shall inform them," the Aedile said.

Brutus said, "And when at such time they have begun to cry out what we have ordered them to cry out, let them not cease, but with a confused din force the immediate execution of whatever punishment we happen to sentence Coriolanus to."

"Very well," the Aedile said.

Sicinius said, "Make them be strong, and make them be ready for this cue whenever we happen to give it to them."

"Go and do these things," Brutus said.

The Aedile exited.

Brutus said, "Let's immediately make him angry. He has been used always to conquer, and to have his pennyworth of answering back. Once he is angry, he cannot be reined again and returned to temperance. Once he is angry, he speaks what's in his heart; and what is in his heart seems likely — with our help — to break his neck."

Sicinius looked up and said, "Well, here he comes."

Coriolanus, Menenius, and Cominius, along with Senators and other patricians, walked into the marketplace.

"Speak calmly, I beg you," Menenius said to Coriolanus.

"Yes, like an hostler, a stableman, who for the poorest coin will endure being called a knave so many times that it would fill up the pages of a book," Coriolanus replied to Menenius.

He then said loudly so all could hear him, "May the honored gods keep Rome safe, and may they keep the chairs of justice occupied by worthy men! May they plant love among us! May they fill our large temples with the ceremonies of peace, and may they not fill our streets with war!"

"Amen, amen," the first Senator said.

"That is a noble wish," Menenius said.

The Aedile returned, leading the plebeians.

Sicinius ordered, "Draw near, you common people."

"Listen to your Tribunes," the Aedile ordered. "Listen to them. Be quiet, I say!"

"First, hear me speak," Coriolanus said.

The two Tribunes replied, "Well, speak. Quiet, everyone!"

"Shall I be charged any further than this present time?" Coriolanus asked. "Will everything be determined here?"

"I ask you," Sicinius said, "whether you submit yourself to the people's voices. Do you recognize the authority of their officers and are you willing to suffer lawful censure for such crimes as shall be proved upon you?"

Coriolanus paused and then said, "I am willing. I agree to all of those things."

"Citizens," Menenius said, "Coriolanus says that he is willing. Consider the military service he has done in war, and think upon the wounds his body bears, which show like graves in the holy churchyard."

"It is as if I were scratched by briers," Coriolanus said. "They are scars that will make people laugh, not cry."

Menenius said, "Consider further, that when he speaks not like a citizen, you find him like a soldier: Do not take his rougher accents for malicious sounds, but as I say, take them as being such as become a soldier, rather than as showing malice toward you."

"Well, well, say no more," Cominius said.

Coriolanus asked, "Why is it that having been elected Consul with all your votes, I am so dishonored that the very same hour I was made Consul you take the Consulship away from me?"

"You answer to us," Sicinius said. "We do not answer to you. We will ask the questions. You are the one on trial."

"Speak, then," Coriolanus replied. "It is true that I ought to answer the charges. That is why I am here."

Sicinius said, "We charge that you have contrived to take from Rome all established political offices and you have contrived to insinuate yourself into possession of a tyrannical power. On account of these actions, you are a traitor to the people."

Instantly angry, Coriolanus said, "What! Traitor!"

"Speak temperately," Menenius said. "Remember your promise."

"May the fires in the lowest Hell enfold the common people!" Coriolanus said to Sicinius. "You call me their traitor, you insulting Tribune! If twenty thousand deaths sat within your eyes, and if your hand clutched as many millions of deaths, and if in your lying tongue were both numbers of deaths, I would say 'You lie' to you with a voice as freely, openly, and frankly as I pray to the gods."

"Do you hear this, people?" Sicinius asked.

"To the rock, to the rock with him!" the plebeians shouted.

They wanted the death penalty for Coriolanus.

"Quiet!" Sicinius ordered. "We do not need to add new charges against him. What you have seen him do and heard him speak — beating your officers, cursing yourselves, opposing laws with strokes of his sword, and here defying those whose great power must try him — even this, which is so criminal that it is worthy of the death penalty, deserves the most extreme death."

Brutus said, "But since he has served Rome well —"

"What are you babbling about service?" Coriolanus asked.

"I am talking about something that I know," Brutus said.

"You?" Coriolanus asked.

Brutus was saying that he knew something about civil service, but Coriolanus believed that military service was much more valuable and much more worthy of respect.

"Is this how you keep the promise that you made your mother?" Menenius asked Coriolanus.

"Know, please —" Cominius said.

Coriolanus interrupted, "I'll know no further. Let them pronounce against me the sentence of the steep Tarpeian death, vagabond exile, flaying, being imprisoned and starving to death with only one grain of wheat to eat per day. I would not buy their mercy at the price of one fair word nor check my courage for what they can give, even if I could have it by saying 'Good morning' to them."

Sicinius said, "Inasmuch as he has, as much as in him lies, from time to time shown malice against the people, seeking means to pluck away their power, and he has now at last given hostile strokes of his sword, not only in the presence of dreaded justice, but also on the ministers who distribute that justice, we immediately banish him in the name of the people and in the power of us the Tribunes from our city. He must never again enter our gates of Rome or he will be thrown down from the Tarpeian cliff. In the people's name, I say it shall be so."

The plebeians shouted, "It shall be so! It shall be so! Let him leave Rome! He's banished, and it shall be so!"

Cominius said, "Hear me, my masters, and my common friends —"

"Coriolanus has been sentenced; there's nothing more to be heard," Sicinius said.

"Let me speak," Cominius said. "I have been Consul, and I can show for Rome her enemies' marks upon me. I love my country's good with a respect more tender, more holy and profound, than my own life, my dear wife's reputation, her womb's increase and treasure of my loins — our children. Then if I would speak that —"

"We know your drift," Sicinius said. "Speak what?"

"There's no more to be said, except that Coriolanus is banished," Brutus said, "as an enemy to the people and his country. It shall be so: He shall leave Rome."

"It shall be so!" the plebeians shouted. "It shall be so!"

"You common cry — pack — of curs!" Coriolanus shouted. "I hate your breath as I hate the reeking vapor of the rotten swamps! I prize your friendship as I prize the dead carcasses of unburied men that corrupt my air! I BANISH YOU! I allow you to remain here with your uncertainty! Let every feeble rumor shake your hearts! Let your enemies, with the nodding of the plumes on their helmets fan you into despair! Continue to have the power to banish your defenders until the only ones left are you, who are enemies to yourselves! Eventually, your ignorance, which you won't know you have until you experience its effects, will deliver you as very abject and humbled captives to some nation that won you without a battle — without blows!

"Despising, because of you, this city of Rome, thus I turn my back. There is a world elsewhere."

Coriolanus exited. With him went Cominius, Menenius, the Senators, and the other patricians.

The Aedile shouted, "The common people's enemy is gone! He is gone!"

"Our enemy is banished!" the plebeians shouted. "He is gone! Yea! Yea!"

They threw their hats into the air.

Sicinius said, "Go, see him exit through the city gates, and follow him, as he has followed you, with all disdain and scorn. Give him deserved vexation and torment. Let a guard go with us through the city to protect us if need be from the patricians."

"Come on! Come on!" the plebeians shouted. "Let's see him exit through the city gates. Come on! May the gods preserve our noble Tribunes! Come on!"

CHAPTER 4

— 4.1 —

Coriolanus, Volumnia, Virgilia, Menenius, Cominius, and the young nobles of Rome stood in front of the city gates. The young, as opposed to the old, nobles of Rome especially supported Coriolanus.

Coriolanus said to his family and friends, "Come, set aside your tears. Let's have a brief farewell: The beast with many heads — the plebeians — butts me away. Mother, where is your long-established courage? You were always accustomed to say that a crisis was the trier of spirits, that common men could bear common chances, that when the sea was calm all boats alike showed mastership in floating. You were always accustomed to say that after suffering a grievous wound, acting as if one were gently wounded required a noble cunning. You were always accustomed to load me with precepts that would make invincible the heart that memorized and learned them."

"Oh, Heavens! Oh, Heavens!" his wife, Virgilia, cried.

"No, please, woman —" Coriolanus began to say.

Volumnia interrupted, "Now may the red pestilence — typhus — strike all tradesmen in Rome, and may all occupations perish!"

"What! What! What!" Coriolanus said. "I shall be loved when I am missed. No, mother, resume that spirit you had when you were accustomed to say that if you had been the wife of Hercules, you would have done six of his twelve labors and saved your husband so much sweat.

"Cominius, do not droop. Adieu.

"Farewell, my wife, and my mother. I'll do well yet.

"You old and true Menenius, your tears are saltier than a younger man's, and the salt is venomous to your eyes.

"My sometime General, I have seen you stern, and you have often beheld heart-hardening spectacles. Tell these sad women that it is as foolish to bewail strokes that cannot be avoided as it is to laugh at them.

"My mother, you know well my hazards have always been your solace; you have always enjoyed the risks I have faced. Believe this and don't take it lightly: Although I go alone, like a lonely dragon that makes his swamp feared and talked about more than seen — your son will either exceed the commonplace and do something remarkable or else he will be caught with cautelous — crafty and deceitful — baits and plots."

"My first son," Volumnia said, "where will you go? Take good Cominius with you for a while. Determine on some course of action to follow rather than expose yourself to each chance event that arises in the way before you."

"Oh, the gods!" Coriolanus said, exasperated because his mother was worrying excessively about him.

"I'll go with you for a month and plan with you where you shall rest and reside so that you may hear from us and we may hear from you," Cominius said. "That way, if the time thrusts forth an occasion when your exile is repealed, we shall not send over the vast world to seek a single man, and lose the opportunity to bring you home. Otherwise, the opportunity will cool in the absence of the person who needs the opportunity, and Rome may decide not to allow you to return from exile."

"Fare you well," Coriolanus said to Cominius. "You have too many years upon you and you are too full of the wars' excesses to go roving with one who is yet unbruised. Accompany me only to the gate."

Coriolanus was, of course, "bruised." He had many scars from his war wounds.

Coriolanus continued, "Come, my sweet wife, my dearest mother, and my friends who have been tested and have been found noble. When I am outside the gate, bid me farewell, and smile. Please, come with me to the gate.

"While I remain above the ground, you shall always hear from me, and you shall never hear of me anything but what is like me formerly. I shall not change."

"What you have said is worthy, as any ear can hear," Menenius said. "Let's not weep. If I could shake off just seven years from my old arms and legs, I swear by the good gods that I would accompany you every foot of your exile."

"Give me your hand," Coriolanus said. "Come."

<h1 style="text-align:center">— 4.2 —</h1>

Sicinius, Brutus, and an Aedile met on a street in Rome.

Sicinius ordered the Aedile, "Tell the plebeians all to go home; Coriolanus has gone, and we'll go no further. The nobility are vexed; they have sided with Coriolanus."

"Now that we have shown our power," Brutus said, "let us seem humbler after it is done than when it was happening. We have gotten what we wanted, and so there is no need for us to make more enemies and to make our enemies more bitter by flaunting our power."

"Tell the plebeians to go home," Sicinius said. "Say that their great enemy is gone, and they have stood strong with their earlier strength."

"Dismiss them and tell them to go home," Brutus said.

The Aedile exited.

Brutus looked up and said, "Here comes Coriolanus' mother."

"Let's not meet her," Sicinius said.

"Why?" Brutus asked,

"They say she's so mad that she's insane."

"They have seen us," Brutus said. "Keep walking."

It was too late for them to escape. Volumnia, Virgilia, and Menenius quickly walked over to the two Tribunes.

Volumnia said, "Oh, you're well met. May the plague that the gods hoard until it is time to punish evildoers be your recompense for the 'friendship' you have shown to Coriolanus!"

"Quiet! Quiet!" Menenius said. "Don't be so loud."

Volumnia said, "If I could speak despite my weeping, you should hear — actually, you shall hear some of what I have to say to you."

Brutus attempted to leave, but Volumnia blocked his way and said, "Do you want to be gone? That is not going to happen."

Sicinius attempted to leave, but Virgilia blocked his way and said, "You shall stay, too. I wish I had the power to say the same thing to my husband."

"Are you acting like men?" Sicinius asked.

Volumnia replied, "Yes, fool; is that a shame? Listen, fool. Wasn't a man my father? Did you have foxship — cunning ingratitude — enough to banish

Coriolanus, who struck more blows for Rome than you have spoken words? Each of us has his or her own heritage."

"Oh, blessed Heavens!" Sicinius said.

"Coriolanus had more noble blows than you ever had wise words, and those blows were for Rome's good," Volumnia said. "I'll tell you what — but I will let you go. ... No, I won't — you shall stay, after all, and listen to me. I wish my son were in Arabia, and your tribe were before him as he held his good sword in his hand."

"What about it?" Sicinius asked.

"What about it!" Virgilia said. "He would make an end of your posterity. In Arabia, he would not have to obey Roman law, and he would kill all your descendants."

"Bastards and all," Volumnia said. "Coriolanus is a good man — consider the wounds that he bears because he fought for Rome!"

"Come, come, peace," Menenius said.

Sicinius said, "I wish that Coriolanus had continued to serve his country as he began, and that he had not unknot by himself the noble knot he made."

The knot was a bond between Coriolanus and Rome.

"I wish he had," Brutus said

"You wish he had!" Volumnia said. "It was you two Tribunes who incensed the rabble against him. You cats! You can judge as fitly of his worth as I can of those mysteries that Heaven will not allow the Earth to know."

"Please, let us go," Brutus said.

"Now, please, sir, get you gone," Volumnia said. "You have done a 'brave' deed. Before you go, hear this: As far as the Capitol exceeds the meanest house in Rome, so far my son — this lady's husband here, this lady, do you see — whom you have banished, exceeds you all."

"Well, well, we'll leave you," Brutus said.

"Why are we staying here to be tormented by someone who lacks her wits?" Sicinius said.

"Take my 'prayers' with you," Volumnia said.

The Tribunes exited.

Volumnia said, "I wish that the gods had nothing else to do but to confirm my curses and bring them about! If I could see my curses being carried out once a day, it would unclog my heart of what lies heavy in it."

Clogs were heavy pieces of wood attached to prisoners to keep them from running away.

"You have told them home truths," Menenius said, "and indeed you have cause to curse them. You'll dine with me?"

"Anger is my food," Volumnia said. "I dine on myself, and so I shall starve with feeding."

In this culture, "to starve" meant 1) "to die" as well as 2) "to be very hungry." Therefore:

1) "I dine on myself, and so I shall die with feeding" meant "I shall consume myself with anger until I die."

2) "I dine on myself, and so I shall be very hungry with feeding" meant "I consume myself with anger, and if I eat food, I will feel better and starve my anger by no longer feeling angry." The implication was that she would not eat food in order to prevent the possibility that eating food would lessen her anger.

"Come, let's go," Volumnia said. "Leave behind this faint whimpering. Instead, lament as I do; I am like Juno in my anger."

Juno was the wife of Jupiter, King of the gods. Her anger was implacable. In mythology, a contest was held to determine which goddess — Juno, Venus, or Minerva — was the most beautiful; Paris, Prince of Troy, judged that beauty contest. Juno lost the contest, and thereafter she hated the Trojans. Her anger was so implacable that she also hated the Romans because Aeneas, a Trojan who had survived the fall of Troy, made his way to Italy and became an important ancestor of the Roman people.

Volumnia said, "Come, come, come."

Menenius said, "Damn! Damn! Damn!"

A Roman and a Volscian met on a road between Rome and Antium.

"I know you well, sir," the Roman said, "and you know me. Your name, I think, is Adrian."

"That is right, sir," the Volscian replied. "Truly, I have forgotten you."

"I am a Roman; and my services are, as your services are, employed against the Romans. Do you know me now?"

"Are you Nicanor?" the Volscian asked.

"Yes, I am he, sir," the Roman replied.

"You had a bigger beard when I last saw you, but your face is well corroborated by your tongue. What's the news in Rome? I have a note from the Volscian state telling me to seek you out there. Our meeting now has saved me a day's journey."

"There have been in Rome strange insurrections," the Roman said. "The common people have opposed themselves against the Senators, patricians, and nobles."

"You say 'has been'! Is it ended, then? Our government does not think so. The Volscians are preparing for war, and they hope to come upon the Romans in the heat of their division."

"The main blaze of it is past, but a small thing would make it flame again," the Roman said. "The nobles are so taking to heart the banishment of that worthy Coriolanus that they are in a ripe readiness to take all power from the people and to pluck from them their Tribunes forever. This lies glowing, I can tell you, and is almost mature for the violent breaking out. The insurrection can break out in violence again at any time."

"Coriolanus has been banished!" the Volscian said.

"Yes, he has been banished, sir."

"You will be welcome in Antium with this intelligence, Nicanor."

"The day serves well for the Volscians now," the Roman said. "I have heard it said that the fittest time to corrupt a man's wife is when she's fallen out with her husband. Your noble Tullus Aufidius will appear well in these wars because his great opponent, Coriolanus, is now no longer wanted by his country."

"Aufidius cannot choose other than to appear well in these wars," the Volscian said. "With Coriolanus gone, Aufidius will certainly triumph. I am very fortunate that I have accidentally encountered you. You have ended my business, and I will merrily accompany you home."

"I shall, between this time and suppertime, tell you very strange things that are going on in Rome, all tending to the good of the Romans' adversaries. Did you say that your government has an army ready?"

"It is a very royal army," the Volscian said. "The military centurions and their soldiers, individually enrolled, already taken into service and on the payroll, are ready to be on foot and marching at an hour's warning."

"I am filled with joy to hear of their readiness, and I am the man, I think, who shall set them on to immediate action," the Roman said. "So, sir, we are heartily well met, and I am very glad to have your company."

"You take my words from me, sir," the Volscian said. "I have the most cause to be glad of your company."

"Well, let us go together," the Roman said.

Wearing ragged clothing, in disguise, and with his face partially hidden, Coriolanus stood in front of Aufidius' house in Antium. He did not know he was standing in front of Aufidius' house.

He said to himself, "A good-looking city is this Antium. City, it is I who made your widows. I have heard many an heir of these beautiful buildings groan and drop in the face of my onslaughts. I hope that no one recognizes me, lest your widowed wives with kitchen spits and boys with stones slay me in petty battle."

A citizen of Antium appeared.

Coriolanus said to him, "May God save you, sir."

"And you," the citizen replied.

"Direct me, if you will, to where great Aufidius resides. Is he in Antium?"

"He is, and he is feasting the nobles of the state at his house this night," the citizen replied.

"Which is his house, please?"

"This one here in front of you."

"Thank you, sir," Coriolanus said. "Farewell."

The citizen exited.

Coriolanus said to himself, "Oh, world, you have slippery, fickle turns of fortune! People who are firmly sworn friends now, whose double — both two and duplicitous — chests seem to wear one heart, whose house, whose bed, whose meal, and whose exercise, are always together, who twin, as it were, in inseparable friendship, shall within this hour, because of a quarrel over an eighth of a penny, break out into bitterest enmity.

"And people who are the fellest — mightiest — foes, whose passions and whose plots have broken their sleep and made them stay awake, each of them thinking how to take the other, will by some chance or some trifle not worth an egg become dear friends and both will join their interests together and have their children unite the two families through marriage.

"So it is with me. I hate my birthplace, which is Rome, and now I love this enemy town, which is Antium. I'll enter this house and talk to Aufidius. If he slays me, he does what is fair and just. But if he gives me the opportunity, I'll do his country service."

Inside Aufidius' house, servants were serving the feast for Aufidius' guests.

The first servant called out, "Wine, wine, wine! What service is here! I think our fellow servants are asleep!"

The second servant called out, "Where's Cotus? My master is calling for him. Cotus!"

Coriolanus walked into the room and said, "This is a good house. The feast smells good, but I don't look like a guest."

In fact, he looked like a beggar because of his disguise and the ragged clothing he was wearing.

The first servant saw Coriolanus and said to him, "What do you want, friend? Where have you come from? This is no place for you. Please, go to the door and wait with the other beggars for handouts."

Coriolanus said to himself, "I have deserved no better reception than this because I am Coriolanus."

Noticing Coriolanus, who was still present, the second servant said to him, "Where have you come from? Is the porter blind? He must be if he allows such fellows as you to enter the house. Please, go outside."

"Go away!" Coriolanus, whose bearing was that of a proud noble, not of a humble beggar, said.

"Me go away!" the second servant said. "You go away!"

"Now you are being troublesome to me," Coriolanus said.

"Are you so brave?" the second servant replied. "I'll have you talked with immediately."

A third servant entered. Seeing Coriolanus, he asked the first servant, "What fellow's this? Who is he?"

"As strange a fellow as I ever looked on," the first servant said. "I cannot get him out of the house. Please, call my master to come and speak to him."

The third servant said to Coriolanus, "What business have you to do here, fellow? Please, leave the house."

"Let me just stand here," Coriolanus said. "I will not hurt your hearth."

"Who are you?" the third servant asked.

"A gentleman," Coriolanus said.

Looking at Coriolanus' ragged clothing, the third servant said, "You are a marvelously poor gentleman."

"That is true," Coriolanus said. "I am."

"Please, poor gentleman," the third servant said, "take up some other station; here's no place for you. Please, leave this house."

"Do what work you have to do," Coriolanus said. "Go, and get fat on cold leftovers."

He pushed the third servant away.

"Won't you leave?" the third servant asked.

He said to the second servant, "Please, tell my master what a strange guest he has here."

"I shall," the second servant said.

He exited to go speak to Aufidius.

The third servant asked Coriolanus, "Where do you dwell?"

"Under the canopy," Coriolanus replied, referring to the canopy of stars at night.

"Under the canopy!" the third servant said.

"Yes."

"Where's that?" the third servant asked. Canopies can be also be ornamental cloths that are hung over beds, so the third servant was not sure what Coriolanus meant by "under the canopy."

Coriolanus replied, "The city of kites and crows."

Kites and crows are predatory birds. Coriolanus may have been referring to the wilderness where he slept, or he may have been referring to Rome, which now he hated because of the predatory Tribunes, or he may have been referring to both.

"In the city of kites and crows!" the third servant said. "What an ass it is — what an ass you are! Then you dwell with proverbially stupid jackdaws, too?"

Coriolanus said, "No, I don't serve your master."

Coriolanus meant that the jackdaws, aka fools, were the servants, but the third servant thought that he meant that the master — Aufidius — was a jackdaw, aka fool.

The third servant said, "What, sir! Do you meddle with my master?"

The third servant used "meddle" in the sense of "have anything to do with," but a slang meaning of "meddle" was "have sex with." Coriolanus used the word in that sense in his next sentence.

Coriolanus said, "Yes, it is a more honest service than to meddle with your lady boss, Aufidius' wife. You babble, and you babble. Go and serve food with your serving platter, and get out of here!"

Coriolanus hit him, and the third servant ran out of the room.

The second servant returned with Aufidius. The third servant exited to perform a task.

Aufidius said, "Where is this fellow?"

"Here, he is, sir," the second servant replied, pointing to Coriolanus. "I would have beaten him like a dog, except that it would have disturbed the lords within."

Although they had fought each other face to face in battle, Aufidius did not recognize Coriolanus. In battle, they had worn helmets.

"Where have you come from?" Aufidius asked the disguised Coriolanus. "What do you want? What is your name? Why don't you speak? Speak, man. Tell me your name."

In his answer, Coriolanus called Aufidius by his praenomen — his first, personal name: Tullus. This is remarkably familiar. Usually, only intimate friends and family would use the praenomen.

Coriolanus revealed his face, which had been partially covered up, and said, "If, Tullus, you still do not know who I am, and, seeing me, do not think that I am the man I am, necessity commands me to tell you my name."

Not recognizing him, Aufidius asked, "What is your name?"

"It is a name that is unmusical to the Volscians' ears, and it is harsh in sound to your ears."

"Tell me, what's your name?" Aufidius asked again. "You have a grim appearance, and your face is commanding. Although your tackle's torn, you show that you are a noble vessel."

Aufidius was speaking metaphorically. Tackle is a ship's rigging, and a vessel is both a ship and the container of a soul. Aufidius was saying that although Coriolanus' clothing was torn, he was obviously a fine man.

Aufidius asked again, "What's your name?"

"Prepare your eyebrows to frown," Coriolanus said. "Don't you know yet who I am?"

"I don't know who you are. What is your name?"

"My name is Caius Martius, who has done to you in particular and to all the Volscians in general great hurt and mischief; evidence of that can be seen in my surname, which is Coriolanus: the conqueror of Corioli. The painful and painstaking service, the extreme dangers and the drops of blood I have shed for my thankless country are requited only with that surname; my surname is a good memorial, and it is evidence for the malice and displeasure that you should bear me.

"Only that name remains to me. Rome's dastardly nobles permitted the common people to indulge their cruelty and envy. All of Rome's nobles have forsaken me, and they have devoured the rest of what I had. They allowed the voices of slaves to whoop me out of Rome. I was tormented as I left Rome to enter exile; it was as if the common people were hunting me.

"Now this crisis has brought me to your hearth, not out of hope — don't mistake my intention — to save my life, for if I had feared death, of all the men in the world I would have avoided you; instead, I have come here out of absolute spite. I want to fully repay those people who banished me, and that is why I stand here before you.

"If you have a vengeful heart within you, a vengeful heart that will revenge the wrongs committed against you and will stop those shameful injuries seen throughout your country, then immediately take action and make my misery serve your purposes. Use my misery so that my revengeful services may prove to be benefits to you, for I will fight against my corrupted country with the temper and passion of all the devils in Hell.

"But if it happens that you dare not do this and you are too tired to try any more your fortunes in war, then in a word I say that I am too weary to love being any longer in this world, and so I present my throat to you and to your long-established hatred of me. In this case, if you don't cut my throat, you would show that you are just a fool, since I with hatred have always sought to meet you on the battlefield, have drawn barrels of blood out of your countrymen's chests, and I cannot live but to your shame, unless I live to do you service."

"Oh, Martius, Martius!" Aufidius replied. "Each word you have spoken has weeded from my heart a root of long-established malice.

"Even if Jupiter should speak divine things from yonder cloud, thundering to say that all you have said is true, I would not believe his thunder more than I would believe you, all-noble Martius.

"Let me twine my arms about your body, against which my grainy ash-wood spear a hundred times has broken against your armor and scarred the Moon with splinters."

At this point, two former enemies became allies. A man who had loved Rome now hated Rome, and a man who had hated Coriolanus now loved Coriolanus. Such things are unusual, as is scarring the Moon, whose goddess is the virgin Diana, with splinters, which are phallic symbols.

Aufidius continued, "Here and now I hug the anvil of my sword — I have swung my sword against your armored body so many times that it is as if I were a blacksmith hammering a sword on an anvil.

"I will contend as hotly and as nobly with your love and friendship as ever in ambitious strength I contended against your valor.

"You should know first, you first of all men, that I loved the maiden I married; never did a man sigh truer breath. But I see you here, you noble thing, and my rapt heart dances more than when I first saw my wedded wife step across my threshold.

"Why, you Mars, you god of war! I tell you that we have an army on foot; and I had intended once more to hew your shield from your brawny arm or lose my arm in attempting to do it.

"You have thoroughly beaten me in battle twelve separate times, and I have each night since dreamed of encounters between yourself and me. In my sleep, we have been down on the ground wrestling together, unbuckling helmets, grabbing each other's throat with our fists, and I have awakened half dead with nothing.

"Worthy Martius, if we had no quarrel with Rome, except that you have been banished from it, we would muster into our army all our males from age twelve to age seventy, and like a bold flood overwhelming its banks we would pour war into the bowels of ungrateful Rome.

"Oh, come with me, go inside the great hall, and take our friendly Senators by the hands. They now are here, taking their leaves of me; I am prepared to march against your territories, although not to march against Rome itself."

Coriolanus said, "You bless me, gods!"

Aufidius said, "Therefore, most perfect sir, if you will have the leading of your own revenge, take one half of my commission and my soldiers, and set down — as best as your experience tells you, since you know your country's strength and weakness — your plan in your own way. Decide whether to knock against the gates of Rome, or violently visit them in their remote territories in order to frighten them before you destroy them. But come to the dining hall. Let me present and commend you first to those who shall say yes to your desires. A thousand welcomes! And you are more a friend now than you ever were an enemy, although, Martius, you were quite an enemy. Give me your hand. You are very welcome!"

Coriolanus and Aufidius exited.

The first servant said, "Here's a strange alteration in their relationship!"

"By my hand," the second servant said, "I had thought to have struck Coriolanus with a cudgel, and yet my mind warned me that his clothes were making a false report of him. My mind warned me that he was not a beggar, although he was dressed in rags."

"What an arm he has!" the first servant said, "He turned me around with his finger and his thumb, just like someone would set a top spinning."

The second servant said, "I knew by his face that there was something in him: He had, sir, a kind of face, I thought — I don't know how to describe it."

"He did have such a face," the first servant said. "He looked as it were — I wish I would be hanged if I didn't think there was more in him than I could think."

"So thought I, I'll be sworn," the second servant said. "He is simply the rarest man in the world."

"I think he is," the first servant said, "but a greater soldier than he you know of."

"Who, my master?" the second servant said.

The servants were starting to compare Coriolanus and their master: Aufidius. Coriolanus was the better soldier, but the servants were reluctant to admit that, lest they get in trouble, so they praised Aufidius as well. They discussed the two men cautiously, using "he" and "him" rather than names in case they were overheard. Such use of pronouns leads to ambiguity. "Our General," however, is not ambiguous; it refers to Aufidius.

"It's not important," the first servant said. "It doesn't matter."

"He is worth six of him," the second servant said.

"That's not true," the first servant said, "but I take him to be the greater soldier."

"Truly, one cannot tell how to say that," the second servant said. "For the defense of a town, our General is excellent."

"Yes, and for an assault, too," the first servant said.

The third servant arrived and said, "Oh, slaves, I can tell you news — news, you rascals!"

The other servants said, "What is it? Tell us."

"I would not be a Roman, of all nations," the third servant said. "I would just as soon be a man condemned to die."

"Why?" the other two servants asked.

"Why, here is the man who was accustomed to thwack — beat — our General."

"Why do you say 'thwack our General'?" the first servant said.

The third servant, worried about getting into trouble for dispraising Aufidius, said, "I do not say 'thwack our General,' but he was always good enough for him."

The second servant said, "Come, we are fellows and friends: We can talk openly."

Although the second servant felt that the servants could speak openly to each other about the respective merits of Coriolanus and Aufidius, he continued to use the pronouns "he" and "him," rather than names: "He was always too hard for him; I have heard him say so himself."

The first servant said, "He was too hard for him, to say the plain truth. Before Corioli he slashed him and notched him like a piece of meat about to be cooked."

The second servant said, "If he had been a cannibal, he could have broiled and eaten him, too."

"What other news do you bring?" the first servant asked.

The third servant said, "Why, he is made so much of here within, it is as if he were the son and heir to Mars, the god of war. He sits at the upper end of the table in a place of honor. The Senators don't ask him a question without first taking off their hats as a mark of respect. Our General himself treats him as if he were a mistress. Our General himself sanctifies himself by touching his guest's hand — it's as if his guest were sacred. Our General himself also rolls his eyes in admiration of his guest's conversation.

"But the bottom — the conclusion — of the news is that our General is cut in the middle and is now only one half of what he was yesterday because now his guest has the other half, by the entreaty and grant of the whole table. He'll go, he says, and drag the porter of the gate of Rome by the ears. He will mow all down before him, and leave the ground over which he passes stripped bare."

The second servant said, "And he's as likely to do it as any man I can imagine."

"Do it!" the third servant said. "He will do it because, you see, sir, he has as many friends as enemies. These friends, sir, as it were, dare not, you see, sir, show themselves, as we term it, his friends while he's in directitude."

The third servant had perhaps meant to say "dis-rectitude," which would mean "a state of unrighteousness." Certainly, in Rome Coriolanus was in a state of disgrace.

"Directitude!" the first servant said, "What's that?"

The third servant ignored the question and said, "But when they shall see, sir, his crest up again, and the man in blood, they will run out of their burrows, like rabbits after a rain, and all will revel with him."

Coriolanus' crest would be up like that of a fighting cock; he would not be crestfallen. "In blood" was a hunting term meaning "in full vigor and cry."

"When will this happen?" the first servant asked.

"Tomorrow, today, immediately," the third servant said. "The war drum will be struck up this afternoon: It is, as it were, a part of their feast, and it will be done before they wipe their lips."

The second servant said, "Why, then we shall have a stirring world again. This peace is good for nothing except to rust iron, increase tailors, and breed ballad-makers."

Tailors had the reputation of being cowardly and effeminate. The second servant was saying that peace tended to breed such men.

The first servant said, "Let me have war, say I. War exceeds peace as much as day exceeds night; it is full of spritely walking — military marching — and it is audible with military music, and it is full of vent."

One meaning of "to vent" was "to get rid of." Earlier, Martius had spoken of venting "musty superfluity." Literally, "musty superfluity" meant "moldy excess food." Metaphorically, it meant "excess people." If the fittest survive, the people who die are not the most fit. For Martius, those people would be the plebeians.

The first servant continued, "Peace is a total paralysis; it is lethargy. Peace is mulled, deaf, sleepy, insensible."

By "mulled," he meant like "like mulled wine." Peace stupefies people.

The first servant continued, "Peace is a begetter of more bastard children than war is a destroyer of men."

The second servant said, "That's true. As war, in some way, may be said to be a plunderer and a rapist, so it cannot be denied that peace is a great maker of cuckolds and unfaithful wives."

"Yes," the first servant said, "and it makes men hate one another."

The third servant said, "The reason that peace makes men hate each other is because in peaceful times they need one another less. For my money, I prefer the wars. I hope to see the lives of Romans regarded as cheap as the lives of Volscians. Lots of us died in the last war; here's hoping lots of them die in this war."

The third servant heard some noise and said, "They are rising from the table; they are rising."

The servants said, "Let's get to work."

Sicinius and Brutus talked together in a public place in Rome.

Sicinius said, "We have not heard anything about Coriolanus, and we need not fear him. The remedy for the disease he caused Rome was the common people, who are now tame and quiet in the present peace of Rome; previously, while Coriolanus was in Rome, the common people were wildly disturbed. Here and now we make his friends blush because the world goes well and peacefully; his friends would rather, even if they themselves suffered by it, behold dissentious numbers of people crowding streets than see our tradesmen working within their shops and going about their proper occupations in a friendly and peaceful fashion."

"We stood up to him at a good time," Brutus said.

He looked up and asked, "Is that Menenius coming toward us?"

"It is he, it is he," Sicinius replied. "Oh, he has grown very friendly to us lately."

"Hail, sir!" the Tribunes said.

"Hail to you both!" Menenius replied.

"Your Coriolanus is not much missed, except by his friends," Sicinius said. "The commonwealth stands, and it would continue to stand even if he were angrier at it."

"All is well," Menenius replied, "and it might have been much better, if Coriolanus could have compromised and become amenable."

"Where is he?" Sicinius asked. "Have you heard?"

"No, I have heard nothing," Menenius replied. "His mother and his wife have also heard nothing from him."

A few citizens walked over to them and said to the two Tribunes, "May the gods preserve you both!"

"Good evening, our neighbors," Sicinius said.

In this culture, evening was anytime after noon.

"Good evening to you all," Brutus said. "Good evening to you all."

The first citizen said, "We ourselves, our wives, and our children, on our knees, are bound to pray for you both."

"Live, and thrive!" Sicinius said to the citizens.

"Farewell, kind neighbors," Brutus said. "We wish that Coriolanus had loved you as we do."

"Now may the gods keep you!" the citizens said.

"Farewell, farewell," the two Tribunes said.

The citizens exited.

"This is a happier and more comely, more graceful time than when these fellows ran about the streets, crying out in confusion," Sicinius said.

"Caius Martius was a worthy officer in the war," Brutus said, "but he was insolent, overcome with pride, ambitious past all thinking, self-loving —"

"And desiring one solitary throne, from which he could rule without assistance or assistants," Sicinius said.

"I don't think that is true," Menenius said.

"We should by this time, to all our lamentations, if Coriolanus had become Consul, found it to be true," Sicinius said.

"The gods have well prevented it, and Rome sits safe and still and quiet without him," Brutus said.

An Aedile walked over to them and said, "Worthy Tribunes, there is a slave, whom we have put in prison, who reports that the Volscians with two separate armies have entered the Roman territories, and with the deepest malice of the war are destroying what lies before them."

"It is Aufidius," Menenius said. "Having heard of our Martius' banishment, he thrusts forth his horns again into the world. When Martius stood up for Rome, Aufidius kept his horns hidden and did not allow them to be seen."

"Why are you talking about Martius?" Sicinius asked.

"Go see to it that this spreader of rumors is whipped," Brutus said. "It cannot be true that the Volscians dare to break the peace treaty they made with us."

"Cannot be true!" Menenius said. "We have it on historical record that it very well can be true, and three times in my lifetime the Volscians have dared to break the peace treaty they made with us.

"But question the fellow rationally before you punish him. Ask him where he heard this, lest you shall chance to whip your source of good information and beat the messenger who bids us to beware of what is in fact to be dreaded."

"Don't tell us that," Sicinius replied. "I know this gossip cannot be true."

"It isn't possible," Brutus said.

A messenger arrived and said to them, "The nobles in great earnestness are all going to the Senate House. Some news has come that changes their countenances."

"It is this slave," Sicinius said. "Go whip him in front of the people's eyes. Nothing but his report is causing this distress."

"Worthy sir," the messenger said, "The slave's report has been corroborated, and more news, more fearsome than the slave's, has been delivered."

"What more fearsome news?" Sicinius asked.

The messenger replied, "It is spoken freely out of many mouths — how probable the news is I do not know — that Martius, who has allied himself with Aufidius, leads an army against Rome, and he vows revenge as spacious as the gulf between the youngest thing and the oldest thing."

"This is most likely!" Sicinius said sarcastically.

"This rumor has been spread only so that the weaker sort may wish good Martius home again," Brutus said.

"That is the trick behind the spreading of this rumor," Brutus said.

"This rumor is unlikely to be true," Menenius said. "Coriolanus and Aufidius can no more be reconciled and be united than can the most violent extremes."

A second messenger arrived and said, "You are sent for to go to the Senate. A fearsome army, led by Caius Martius joined with Aufidius, rages upon our territories, and their soldiers have already overpowered everything in their path, consumed it with fire, and taken what lay before them."

Cominius arrived and said to the two Tribunes, "Oh, you have made 'good' work!"

"What is the news?" Menenius asked. "What is the news?"

Cominius said to the two Tribunes, "You have helped to rape your own daughters, to melt the city leaden roofs upon your heads, to see your wives raped and dishonored in front of your eyes —"

Menenius interrupted, "What is the news? What is the news?"

Cominius continued, "— your temples burned to their foundations, and your rights and liberties, on which you insisted, confined into the tiny hole made by an auger."

An auger is a drilling tool.

"Please, tell us now your news," Menenius said. "You Tribunes have made 'fair' work, I am afraid. Please, Cominius, what is your news? If Martius should have joined with the Volscians —"

Cominius interrupted, "If! Martius is their god: He leads them like a thing made by some deity other than nature, some deity that shapes man better; and the Volscians follow him, against us brats, with no less confidence than boys pursuing summer butterflies or butchers killing flies."

Menenius said to the two Tribunes, "You have made 'good' work, you and your apron-men; you who stood up so much for the votes of workers and the breath of garlic-eaters!"

"Apron-men" were men who worked while wearing aprons; for example, a sword maker would sometimes wear a protective apron. Members of the working class often ate garlic as a spice and because of its medicinal qualities.

Cominius said, "Like an earthquake, he will shake your Rome about your ears."

"Just like Hercules shook down mellow fruit when he retrieved golden apples from the garden of the Hesperides as one of his famous labors," Menenius said. "You Tribunes have made 'fair' work!"

"But is this true, sir?" Brutus asked.

"Yes, it is true," Cominius replied, "and you'll look pale with fear before you find it other than true. All the regions smilingly and joyfully revolt, and all who resist are mocked for valiant ignorance, and they perish as faithful and loyal fools. Who is it can blame Martius? Your enemies and his find something worthwhile and admirable in him."

"We are all ruined and destroyed, unless the noble man has mercy on us," Menenius said.

"Who shall ask for mercy?" Cominius asked. "The Tribunes cannot do it for shame; the people deserve the same kind of 'pity' from him as the wolf deserves from the shepherds. As for his best friends, if they should say now to him, 'Be good to Rome,' they would exhort him even as would those who had deserved his hate, and they therein would show themselves to be like his enemies. Previously, his best friends had not done enough to defend him."

"That is true," Menenius said. "If he were putting to my house the brand of fire that would consume it, I would not have the audacity to say, 'Please, stop.'

You two Tribunes have done a 'fine' job, you and your craftsmen! You craftiness has worked out 'well'!"

Cominius said, "You two Tribunes have brought fear and trembling upon Rome, which has never been so incapable of helping itself."

"Don't say that we brought this fear and trembling upon Rome," the two Tribunes said.

"Why not?" Menenius asked. "Did we patricians do this? We loved Martius, but like beasts and cowardly nobles, we gave way to your mobs of people who hooted him out of the city."

"But I fear they'll roar — in fear — him in again," Cominius said. "Tullus Aufidius, second in fame among men, obeys Coriolanus' every command as if he were his second-in-command. Desperation is all the policy, strength, and defense that Rome can make against them and their armies."

A troop of citizens arrived.

Menenius said, "Here come the mobs. And is Aufidius with Coriolanus? You are the ones who made the air unwholesome, when you threw your stinking greasy hats in the air while hooting at Coriolanus' exile. Now he's coming; and there is not a hair upon one of his soldiers' heads that will not prove to be a whip. As many heads as you threw coxcombs — fools' hats — up in the air will he tumble down and pay you for your votes. It doesn't matter; if he burns us all into one piece of charcoal, we have deserved it."

The citizens said, "Indeed, we hear fearsome news."

The first citizen said, "As for my own part, when I said, 'Banish him,' I said it was a pity."

"And so did I," the second citizen said.

"And so did I," the third citizen said, "and, to say the truth, so did very many of us. What we did, we did for the best, and although we willingly consented to his banishment, yet it was against our will."

"You are 'good' things, you voters!" Cominius said.

"You Tribunes have made 'good' work, you and your cry — pack — of dogs!" Menenius said. "Shall we go to the Capitol?"

"Yes, what else can we do?" Cominius said.

Cominius and Menenius exited. So did the messengers.

Sicinius said to the citizens, "Go, masters, go home. Don't be dismayed. Cominius and Menenius are part of a faction that would be glad to have this news be true that they so pretend to fear. Go home, and show no sign of fear."

"May the gods be good to us!" the first citizen said. "Come, masters, let's go home. I always said that we were in the wrong when we banished Coriolanus."

"So did we all," the second citizen said. "But, come, let's go home."

The citizens exited.

"I do not like this news," Brutus said.

"Nor do I," Sicinius said.

"Let's go to the Capitol," Brutus said. "I would give half my wealth to have this news be a lie!"

"Please, let's go," Sicinius said.

Aufidius and his Lieutenant talked together in their military camp, which was a short distance from Rome.

"Do my soldiers still fly to Coriolanus the Roman?" Aufidius asked.

His Lieutenant answered, "I do not know what witchcraft's in him, but your soldiers use him as the grace before their meal, their talk while sitting at the dining table, and their thanks at the end of the meal. And you are darkened and eclipsed in this military campaign, sir, even by your own soldiers."

"I cannot help it now," Aufidius said, "unless I use means by which I would lame the foot of our design against Rome. He bears himself more proudlier, even to my own person, than I thought he would when I first embraced him, yet his nature in being proud is no changeling: His nature is proud, and he is true to his nature. I must excuse what cannot be amended."

"Yet I wish, sir — I mean as far as you are concerned — that you had not shared your commission with him, but either had led the army by yourself, or else had let him lead the army by himself."

"I understand you well," Aufidius said, "and you may be sure that when Coriolanus comes to his reckoning, he does not know what I can charge against him. Although it seems, and so he thinks it is, and it is no less apparent to the vulgar eye, that he bears all things fairly and shows good management for the Volscian state, fights like a dragon, and achieves victory as soon as he draws his sword, yet he has left undone something that shall break his neck or put at hazard my neck, whenever we come to our reckoning."

The Lieutenant said, "Sir, I ask you, do you think he'll conquer Rome?"

"All places yield to him before he begins a siege, and the young nobility of Rome are on his side. The Senators and older patricians support him, too. The Tribunes are no soldiers, and the Tribunes' people will be as rash in the repeal of his exile as they were hasty to expel him from Rome. I think he'll be to Rome as is the osprey — the fish hawk — to the fish. The fish hawk takes its prey by sovereignty of nature; it is so majestic that fish surrender to it.

"At first Coriolanus was a noble servant to the Romans, but he could not carry his honors equably. Whether it was pride, which always corrupts the fortunate man who enjoys uninterrupted success; whether it was defect of judgment, causing him to fail in the management of those opportunities that he was lord of; or whether it was his nature, which is not to be other than one thing, causing him not to be able to move from the military helmet to the Senatorial cushion, but commanding peace always with the same austere demeanor as he controlled the war ... it is one of these faults — Coriolanus has touches of all these faults ... just a touch, not the entire vice, for I dare to absolve him of that accusation — but it is one of these faults that made him feared, and therefore hated, and therefore banished. But he also has a merit — valor — that makes one choke while pointing out his faults.

"Our virtues lie in the interpretation of the time; how they are regarded depends on how they are interpreted at a particular time. What is a virtue in war may not be a virtue in peace.

"And power, which is in itself most commendable, has not a tomb as obvious and evident as a speaking platform to extol what it has done; extolling one's virtue is a certain way to have that virtue lightly regarded.

"A person who reaches the top of the Wheel of Fortune will soon decline. A powerful person who spends time boasting about his accomplishments instead of accomplishing new things will cease to be powerful. A person who writes his autobiography is likely to die soon. After a powerful person dies, people speak good things about him.

"One fire drives out one fire; one nail drives out one nail; Rights by rights falter; strengths by strengths fail. One force can be overpowered by a stronger force of the same kind. The strong man meets a stronger man.

"Come, let's go.

"When, Caius, Rome is yours, then you will be at your poorest, for then you shortly will be mine."

CHAPTER 5
— 5.1 —

Menenius, Cominius, Sicinius, and Brutus talked together in a public place in Rome. Others were present. Previously, Cominius had pleaded with Coriolanus to spare Rome, but he had gotten nowhere.

"No, I'll not go plead to Coriolanus," Menenius said. "You heard what he said to Cominius, who was formerly his General, and who loved him with close personal affection. Coriolanus has called me his father, but what of that?

"Go, you who banished him. A mile before you reach his tent, fall down and walk on your knees to him — that is the way to reach his mercy.

"Since he was reluctant to hear Cominius speak, I'll stay at home."

"He pretended not to know me," Cominius said.

"Do you hear this?" Menenius asked.

"Yet at one time he called me by my name," Cominius said. "I brought up our old friendship, and the drops of blood that we have bled together. He would not answer to the name 'Coriolanus.' He forbade all names. He was a kind of nothing; he seemed to want to be without a title until he had forged for himself a new title out of the fire of burning Rome."

Menenius said to the two Tribunes, "Why, you have done 'good' work! You are a pair of Tribunes who have wrecked Rome in order to make charcoal cheap. People won't need to buy charcoal because they can warm themselves at their own hearth as their house burns down — that is a 'noble accomplishment' you will be remembered for!"

Cominius said, "I reminded Coriolanus how royal it is to pardon someone when a pardon is not expected. He replied that my implied request for him to spare Rome was a barefaced, shameless, paltry petition of a state to one whom the state had punished."

"Very well," Menenius said. "Could he say less?"

"I attempted to awaken his regard for his personal friends," Cominius said. "His answer to me was that he could not take the time to pick them out of a pile of stinky musty chaff. He said that it was folly, for one poor kernel of grain or two, to leave the offensive chaff unburned and so always have to smell it."

Mathew 3:12 speaks of God, Who is good and will gather the kernels of grain: "*Whose fan is in his hand, and he will th[o]roughly purge his floor, and gather his wheat into the garner; but he will burn up the chaff with unquenchable fire*" (King James Version).

Menenius said, "For one poor kernel of grain or two! I am one of those; his mother, his wife, his child, and this worthy fellow Cominius, too — we are the grains.

"You Tribunes are the musty chaff; and your stink is smelled above the Moon and to the high Heavens. We will be burned because of you."

"Please, be calm," Sicinius said. "Even if you refuse to give us your aid in this crisis in which help was never so greatly needed, yet do not upbraid us with our distress. But, surely, if you would be your country's pleader, your good tongue, more than the army we can raise on such short notice, might stop our countryman Coriolanus from attacking Rome."

"No, I'll not meddle in this," Menenius said.

"Please," Sicinius said. "Go to Coriolanus, and plead to him to spare Rome."

"What should I do if I go to him?" Menenius asked.

"Just try and see what your friendship with Martius can do for Rome," Brutus replied.

Menenius said, "Well, let's say that Martius makes me return to Rome, just as he made Cominius return, without having listened to me, what then? I will return to Rome only as an unhappy friend, grief-stricken because of his unkindness. What if this comes to be true?"

"You will still receive thanks from Rome in the full measure of what your good will intended to do," Sicinius said.

"I'll undertake this embassy," Menenius said. "I think he'll hear me out. Still, his biting his lip and rejecting good Cominius much disheartens me."

He thought a moment and then said, "Coriolanus was not approached at the right time; he had not dined. When our veins are unfilled, our blood is cold, and then we pout upon the morning and we are unlikely to give or to forgive, but when we have stuffed the digestive tract and these conveyances of our blood with wine and food, we have suppler, more flexible souls than we have during our priest-like fasts; therefore, I'll watch and wait until he has dined well and so will be amenable to our request, and then I'll talk to him."

"You know the road that leads directly to his kindness, and you cannot lose your way," Brutus said.

"Indeed," Menenius said, "I'll test him, and let the result be what it may. I shall before long have knowledge of the outcome of my going to him."

Menenius exited.

Cominius said, "Coriolanus will never listen to Menenius."

"He won't?" Sicinius asked.

Cominius replied, "I tell you that it's as if Coriolanus sat on a throne of gold, his eyes red and inflamed as if they would burn Rome; and his sense of the injury done to him is the jailer to his sense of pity. I kneeled before him; very faintly he said 'Rise,' and he dismissed me like this" — he demonstrated — "with a wave of his speechless hand. He sent after me a written note detailing what he would do, and what he would not do, what he would concede, and what he would not concede. He has sworn an oath that we must yield to his conditions.

"So now all hope is vain … unless his noble mother and his wife can revive hope. I hear that they intend to solicit him to give mercy to his country. Therefore, let's leave here, and with our fair entreaties hasten them on to visit Coriolanus."

Two guards were stationed at the entrance of the Volscian military camp before Rome. Menenius walked up to them.

"Stop! From where have you come?" the first guard said.

"Stop, and go back where you came from," the second guard ordered.

Menenius said, "You guard like men should; you do well. But with your permission, let me say that I am an officer of state, and I have come to speak with Coriolanus."

"From where have you come?" the first guard asked again.

"From Rome."

"You may not pass, you must return to Rome," the first guard said. Our General will listen no more to anyone who comes from Rome."

"You'll see your Rome embraced with fire before you'll speak with Coriolanus," the second guard said.

"My good friends," Menenius said, "if you have heard your General talk about Rome and about his friends there, it is more than likely that the sound of my name has touched your ears. My name is Menenius."

"Even if that is your name, you must go back to Rome," the first guard said. "The virtue of your name is not here passable and sufficient to get you entry into our camp. Your name is not a password that will gain you entry into our camp."

"I tell you, fellow, the General is my loving friend. I have been the book of his good acts, and in me men have read about his unparalleled name, perhaps amplified and exaggerated, for I have always bolstered my friends, of whom he's the chief, with all the size that truth would allow without collapsing. Indeed, sometimes, like a ball being bowled on a tricky, deceptive green, I have tumbled past the mark, and in his praise I have almost endorsed a falsehood; therefore, fellow, I must have leave to pass."

"Indeed, sir, if you had told as many lies in his behalf as you have uttered words in your own, you would not pass here; no, even if it were as virtuous to lie as to live chastely," the first guard said. "Therefore, go back to Rome."

"Please, fellow, remember that my name is Menenius, and I have always sided with the faction of your General."

"Even if you have lied in his behalf, as you say you have," the second guard said, "I am one who, telling the truth under his command, must say that you cannot pass. Therefore, go back to Rome."

"Has he dined, can you tell me?" Menenius asked. "For I would not speak with him until after dinner."

"You are a Roman, are you?" the first guard asked.

"I am, as your General is," Menenius replied.

"Then you should hate Rome, as he does," the first guard said. "Can you, when you have pushed out your gates the very defender of them, and, in a violent popular ignorance, given your enemy your shield, think to confront his revenges with the easy groans of old women, the virginal, supplicating palms of your daughters, or with the palsied intercession of such a decayed dotant — dotard, dullard, and one who dotes on Coriolanus — as you seem to be? Can you think to blow out the intended fire your city is ready to flame in, with such weak breath as this? No, you are deceived; therefore, go back to Rome, and prepare for your execution. You are condemned: Our General has sworn not to give you reprieve and pardon."

"Sirrah, if your Captain knew I were here, he would treat me with respect," Menenius said.

"Sirrah" was a title used to address someone of a social rank inferior to the speaker.

"Come on, my Captain does not know you," the first guard said.

His Captain was Aufidius.

"I mean, your General," Menenius said.

"My General does not care for you," the first guard said. "Go back to Rome, I say, go. Lest I let make you bleed the last remaining half-pint of blood an old man like you has, go back. That's all that you will get from us guards — the command to go back to Rome."

"But, fellow, fellow —"

Coriolanus and Aufidius arrived; they had heard loud voices.

Coriolanus asked, "What's the matter?"

Menenius said to the first guard, "Now, you rogue, I have news for you. You shall know now that I am held in respect; you shall perceive that a Jack guardant — a rascal guard — cannot use his office to keep me from my son Coriolanus. Judge, after seeing how he receives me, whether you risk being hanged or suffering some other death that will take longer and involve crueler suffering. Look at what happens now, and faint in fear of what's going to happen to you."

Menenius then said to Coriolanus, "May the glorious gods sit in hourly synod about your particular prosperity, and may they love you no worse than your old father Menenius does!

"Oh, my son, my son! You are preparing fire for us. Look at my tears — here's water to quench the fire. I was only with great difficulty persuaded to come to you, but being assured none but myself could move you, I have been blown out of your Roman gates with sighs; and solemnly and earnestly appeal to you to pardon Rome and your imploring countrymen. May the good gods assuage your wrath, and turn the dregs of it upon this varlet guard here — this guard, who, like a blockhead and an obstacle, has denied my access to you."

"Go away!" Coriolanus ordered.

"What! Go away?" Menenius said.

"Wife, mother, child, I know none of them," Coriolanus said. "My affairs are made subservient to the affairs of others. Although I am personally responsible for my revenge, my ability to grant remissions belongs to the Volscians.

"That we have been familiar friends, ungrateful forgetfulness — at first Rome's and now mine — shall poison our friendship, rather than pity shall note and remember how much we have been friends. Therefore, be gone. My ears against your petitions to me are stronger than your Roman gates are against my army. Yet, because I was your friend, take this letter along with you. I wrote it for your sake."

Coriolanus gave Menenius a letter and then continued, "I would have sent it to Rome. I will not hear you speak another word, Menenius."

He then said, "Aufidius, this man was my beloved friend in Rome, yet you see how I treat him now!"

"You have a resolute mind," Aufidius said.

Coriolanus and Aufidius exited.

"Now, sir, is your name Menenius?" the first guard asked.

"It is a spell, you see, of much power," the second guard said, sarcastically. "You know the way back to Rome."

"Did you hear how we are scolded for keeping your greatness away from Coriolanus?" the first guard asked.

"What reason, do you think, I have to faint out of fear?" the second guard asked.

Menenius replied, "I care neither for the world nor for your General. As for such things as you, I can scarcely think there are any since you are so slight. He who has a will to commit suicide and die by his own hand does not fear death from the hands of another person. Let your General do his worst. As for you, be what you are, live for a long time, and may your misery increase with your age! I tell you, as I was told, go away!"

Menenius exited.

The first guard said, "He was a noble fellow, I'll give him that."

"The worthy fellow is our General," the second guard said. "He's the rock, the oak that is not to be shaken by the wind."

One of Aesop's fables taught the lesson that pride can lead to a fall: "The humble reed that bends in the wind is stronger than the proud oak that breaks in a storm."

Coriolanus, Aufidius, and others met in the Volscian military camp.

Coriolanus said, "Tomorrow we will encamp our army before the walls of Rome. Aufidius, as you are my partner in this action, you must report to the Volscian lords how plainly and openly I have borne this business."

Aufidius acknowledged, "You have respected only the Volscian ends and purposes; you have stopped your ears against the petition of the Roman people; you have never allowed any Roman to make to you a private whisper — no, not even by such friends who thought that you surely would allow them to speak to you."

Coriolanus said, "This last old man, whom with a cracked and broken heart I have sent to Rome, loved me more than a father loves his son; indeed, he made a god of me. The Romans' last resort was to send him, for whose old love I have, although I showed a sour disposition to him, once more offered the conditions I first sent to the Romans, which they refused and cannot now accept as a point of honor. I did that only to show grace to him, who thought he could do more. A very little I have yielded to, but hereafter I will not listen to fresh embassies and suits, neither from the state nor private friends."

He heard a noise and asked, "What shouting is this?"

He guessed the cause of the noise and said to himself, "Shall I be tempted to infringe my vow at the same time it is made? I will not."

Wearing mourning clothing, Virgilia, Volumnia, Valeria, and some attendants arrived. With them was Martius' son, young Martius.

Coriolanus said to himself, "My wife comes foremost; then my mother — the honored mold wherein this trunk of mine was framed — and holding her hand is the grandchild to her blood. But leave me, all affection and emotion! All bond and privilege of human nature, break and get away from me! Let it be virtuous to be obstinate and unyielding.

"What is that curtsy worth? Or those doves' eyes, which can make gods forsworn? I melt, and I am not made of stronger earth than other men. My mother bows to me, as if Olympus, the home of the gods, would nod in supplication to a molehill, and my young boy has a look of intercession, to which great human nature cries, 'Deny it not.'

"Let the Volscians plow Rome and harrow Italy. I'll never be such a gosling as to obey natural instinct, but I will stand firm, as if a man were author and parent of himself and knew no other kin."

Virgilia said, "My lord and husband!"

"These eyes are not the same as those I wore in Rome," Coriolanus replied.

He meant that he had changed and no longer looked at her the same way that he had looked at her previously to being exiled from Rome.

His wife replied, "The sorrow that shows us thus changed makes you think so. Our sorrow has changed us so much that you think you have new eyes."

Coriolanus said to himself, "Like a dull, unintelligent actor now, I have forgotten my part, I am at a loss for words, and I am completely disgraced."

He recovered enough to say, "Best of my flesh, forgive my cruelty, but do not, because I have asked you for your forgiveness, say to me, 'Forgive our Romans.'"

His wife kissed him.

Coriolanus said, "Oh, when I was exiled, you gave me a kiss that has lasted as long as my exile and that is as sweet as my revenge! Now, by the jealous Queen of Heaven, Juno, goddess of marriage and punisher of the unfaithful, I swear that when I left Rome, I carried away that kiss from you, dear; and my true lips have virgined it — been chaste — ever since.

"You gods! I prate, and I leave unsaluted and ungreeted the noblest mother of the world. Sink, my knee, in the earth."

He knelt and said to Volumnia, his mother, "Let my knee do its duty and make a deeper impression in the earth than other sons make so that I can acknowledge my respect for you more than common sons acknowledge their mothers."

His mother replied, "Oh, stand up, blessed one, while with no softer cushion than the flint, I kneel before you and improperly show my maternal respect to you, as I have been 'mistaken' all this while about the respect owed between the child and parent. Previously, I thought that you ought to kneel to show me respect, but now I 'know' that I ought to kneel to show you respect."

This was shocking: A child ought to kneel to show respect to his parent; it is wrong for a parent to kneel to show respect to her child.

"What is this?" a shocked Coriolanus said. "You are on your knees to me! This is a rebuke to me!

"Let the pebbles on the barren beach rise up and strike the stars!

"Let the mutinous winds blow the proud cedars so that they strike against the fiery Sun!

"Let impossibility be murdered, in order to make what is impossible only slight work. Let the laws of nature be destroyed so that impossible things happen!"

Coriolanus valued valor and honor. Suicide can be honorable in some situations. A parent kneeling humbly to her son is not an honorable situation. He stood up and raised his mother.

"You are my warrior," his mother said. "I helped to frame — shape and train — you."

She then asked him, "Do you know this lady?"

The lady was her friend Valeria.

Coriolanus replied, "She is the noble sister of Publicola, an important Roman patrician. She is Rome's Moon, whose goddess is the virgin Diana. She is as chaste as the icicle that's crystalized by the frost from purest snow and hangs on Diana's temple. She is dear Valeria!"

Moving Coriolanus' son forward, Volumnia said, "This boy is a poor miniature of yourself, but with the execution of enough time he may show that he is completely like yourself."

Coriolanus said to his son, "May Mars, the god of soldiers, with the consent of supreme Jove, King of the gods, infuse your thoughts with nobleness so that you may prove to be incapable of dishonor and so that you may prove to stand out in the wars like a great sea-beacon, withstanding every gust of wind, and saving those who see you!"

Volumnia said to Coriolanus' son, "Get on your knee, young sir."

He knelt.

"That's my brave and splendid boy!" Coriolanus said.

"Even he, as well as your wife, this lady, and myself, are petitioners to you," Volumnia said.

"Please, be quiet," Coriolanus said. "Or, if you must ask, remember this before you ask: The thing I have forsworn to grant may never be regarded by you as denials to all of you. I cannot grant what I have sworn not to grant. Do not ask me to dismiss my soldiers, or to bargain and come to terms with Rome's working class.

"Don't tell me in which ways I seem unnatural. Don't try to alleviate my rages and revenges with your colder reasons."

"Oh, say no more, no more!" Volumnia said. "You have said you will not grant us anything, for we have nothing else to ask, except that which you already deny us. Yet we will ask it, so that, if you fail to give us our request, the blame may hang upon your hardness; therefore, hear us out."

Coriolanus said, "Aufidius, and you Volscians, listen, for we'll hear nothing from Rome in private."

He sat down and then asked his mother, "What is your request?"

"Even if we would be silent and not speak, our mourning clothing and the state of our mourning bodies would betray what kind of life we have led since your exile. Think to yourself how much more unfortunate than all living women are we who have come here, since the sight of you, which should make our eyes flow with joy and our hearts dance with comforts, constrains them instead to weep and shake with fear and sorrow because the mother, the wife, and the child see the son, the husband, and the father tearing his country's bowels out.

"And your enmity's most deadly to poor us. You ban us from praying to the gods, which is a comfort that all but we can enjoy. How can we pray for the safety of our country, to which we are bound, and at the same time pray for victory for you, to whom we are also bound? Either we must lose our country, which is our dear nurse, or else we must lose you, who is our comfort in our country. We must find an inevitable calamity, even though we have our wish, whichever side should win: For either you must, as a traitor who helps a foreign power, be led with manacles through our streets, or else you must triumphantly tread on your country's ruin, and bear the palm of victory for having 'bravely' shed the blood of your wife and children.

"As for myself, son, I do not intend to wait on fortune; I will not wait until these wars determine who is victorious. If I cannot persuade you rather to show a noble grace to both countries — that of the Romans and that of the Volscians — than to seek the end of one of those countries, you shall no sooner march to assault your country than you will tread — believe that what I say is true — on your mother's womb that brought you into this world."

She was threatening to commit suicide if he continued to march on Rome.

"Yes, and on my womb, too," Coriolanus' wife said. "My womb that brought forth for you this boy to keep your name living in time."

Coriolanus' young son said, "He shall not tread on me; I'll run away until I am bigger, but then I'll fight."

Coriolanus said, "He who does not want to feel a woman's tenderness must not see a child or a woman's face. I have sat too long."

He stood up.

"No, do not go from us like this," his mother said. "If it were the case that our request did tend to save the Romans, and by so doing destroy the Volscians whom you serve, you might condemn us as being poisonous to your honor. But that is not the case; our suit is that you reconcile the two sides: the Romans and the Volscians. While the Volscians may say, 'This mercy we have shown,' the Romans may say, 'This mercy we have received.' And each person on either side will give the all-hail to you and cry, 'May you be blest for creating this peace!'

"You know, great son, that how a war will end is uncertain, but this is certain: If you conquer Rome, the benefit that you shall thereby reap is such a name whose repetition will be dogged with curses. The history books will have this written in them: 'The man was noble, but with his last attempt at doing a great deed he wiped his nobility out; he destroyed his country, and his name remains abhorred to the ensuing age.'

"Speak to me, son.

"You have sought the fine strains of honor in order to imitate the graces of the gods. You wanted to tear with thunder the wide cheeks of the blowing air."

In maps of the time, illustrations showed wind issuing from the puffed-out cheeks and open mouth of Aeolus, god of the winds.

Volumnia continued, "And you wanted to load your sulphur into a thunderbolt that would split only an oak tree."

In saying that the thunderbolt split an oak tree — rather than a man — she was leading up to an important point: An important grace of the gods is mercy, and that is the grace that her son ought to seek.

Volumnia continued, "Why don't you speak? Do you think it is honorable for a noble man always to remember wrongs?

"Daughter, speak: He does not care that you are weeping.

"Speak, boy. Perhaps your childishness will move him more than can our reasons and arguments.

"There's no man in the world more bound to his mother; yet here he lets me prattle like one publicly humiliated in the stocks."

The stocks were pieces of wood with half-circles carved out of one edge; when two pieces of wood were put together, the half-circles would form circles. A person would be restrained by having his or her feet, hands, and/or head put in the circles. The person being punished might plead, but the people punishing him would ignore his or her pleas.

Volumnia continued, "You have never in your life showed your dear mother any courtesy when she, poor hen, fond of no second brood, has clucked you to the wars and safely back home, loaded with honor. Say my request's unjust, and kick me away, but if my request is just, then you are not honest and honorable, and the gods will plague you because you keep back from me the respect that a child ought to give to a mother."

Coriolanus started to leave.

Volumnia said, "He turns away. Get down on your knees, ladies; let us shame him with our knees. To his surname 'Coriolanus' belongs more pride than pity to our prayers. He is a man of Corioli, not the conqueror of Corioli. Get down, ladies."

The three ladies and Coriolanus' son knelt.

Volumnia continued, "Let's make an end of it. This is the last appeal we will make. And so we will go home to Rome, and die among our neighbors.

"Coriolanus, look at us. This boy, who cannot tell what he wants to have, but who kneels and holds up his hands because we ladies do, argues for our petition with more strength than you have to deny it."

She paused; Coriolanus remained silent.

She then said, "Come, let us go, ladies. This fellow — Coriolanus — had a Volscian for his mother. His wife is in Corioli and his 'child' who is beside me resembles him simply by chance.

"Yet give us our dismissal, Coriolanus. I am hushed until our city is set on fire, and then I'll speak a little."

The little she would speak would be to curse her son as she died.

Coriolanus held her hand; he was silent for a short time.

Then he said, "Oh, mother, mother! What have you done? Behold, the Heavens open, the gods look down, and they laugh at this unnatural scene."

The scene was unnatural because the mother's successful pleading put her son's life at risk.

Coriolanus continued, "My mother! Mother! You have won a happy victory for Rome, but as for your son — believe it, oh, believe it, you have prevailed with him in a way that is very dangerous and perhaps mortal to him. But, let it come.

"Aufidius, although I cannot make true wars, wars that are true to my promise, yet I'll frame a suitable peace. Now, good Aufidius, if you were in my place, would you have heard a mother less? Or granted less, Aufidius?"

Aufidius replied, "I was moved by it."

"I dare to swear that you were," Coriolanus said, "and, sir, it is no little thing to make my eyes sweat compassion."

He was crying.

Coriolanus continued, "But, good sir, advise me what peace treaty you would like to make. As for me, I'll not return to Rome; instead, I'll go back with you. Please, stand by me in this affair.

"Oh, mother! Oh, wife!"

As Coriolanus talked with his wife and his mother, Aufidius said to himself, "I am glad you have set your mercy and your honor at war inside yourself. Out of that I'll manipulate things so that I regain my former fortune."

Coriolanus said to his mother and his wife, "Yes, and soon. But we will drink together, and you shall bear a better witness back to and in Rome in your own person than words. We will give Rome a new peace treaty, which will have fair terms as did the old peace treaty, and which will be counter-signed and sanctioned.

"Come, go inside the tent with us. Ladies, you deserve to have a temple built to you. All the swords in Italy and all her military allies could not have made this peace."

Menenius and Sicinius talked together in a public place in Rome.

Menenius said, "Do you see yonder the corner of the Capitol? Do you see yonder cornerstone?"

"Why, what about it?" Sicinius asked.

"If it is possible for you to move the huge cornerstone with your little finger, then there is some hope that the ladies of Rome, especially his mother, may prevail with Coriolanus. But I say there is no hope for this happening. Our throats are sentenced and wait for execution."

"Is it possible that so short a time can alter the character of a man!" Sicinius asked.

"There is a difference between a grub and a butterfly, yet the butterfly was a grub. This Martius has grown from a man to a dragon. He has wings; he's more than a creeping thing."

"He loved his mother dearly."

"So did he love me," Menenius said, "and he no more remembers his mother now than an eight-year-old horse remembers its dam. The tartness of his face sours ripe grapes. When he walks, he moves like a war machine, and the ground shrinks before his treading. He is able to pierce body armor with his eye. He talks like a death knell, and his expression of disapproval is an assault. He sits in his chair of state as if he were a statue of the Greek conqueror Alexander the Great. What he orders to be done is finished at the same time he finishes commanding it to be done. He lacks nothing that a god has except eternity and a Heaven to be enthroned in."

"He also lacks the mercy of a god, if your report about him is true," Sicinius said.

"I paint his character as it really is. Note what mercy his mother shall bring from him: There is no more mercy in him than there is milk in a male tiger. Our poor city shall find that to be true, and all this is due to you."

"May the gods be good to us!" Sicinius said.

"In such a case the gods will not be good to us," Menenius said. "When we banished Coriolanus, we did not respect the gods, and now that he is returning to break our necks, the gods do not respect us."

A messenger arrived and said to Sicinius, "Sir, if you want to save your life, flee to your house. The plebeians have got Brutus, your fellow Tribune, and they are dragging him up and down, all while swearing that if the Roman ladies do not bring good news home, they'll give him death, killing him slowly, inch by inch."

A second messenger arrived.

Sicinius asked, "What's the news?"

"Good news, good news," the messenger replied. "The ladies have prevailed, the Volscians have left their military camp, and Martius has gone. A merrier day has never yet greeted Rome. No, not even the day when the Tarquins were expelled."

"Friend," Sicinius asked, "are you certain this is true? Is it most certainly true?"

"I am as certain I know this news is true as I am certain I know the Sun is fire," the messenger said, "Where have you been lurking that you doubt this news? The swelling, wind-blown tide never hurried through the arch of a bridge as the relieved people hurry through the gates of Rome to greet the returning ladies. Why, listen!"

Musical instruments could be heard playing loudly in celebration. Romans shouted in joy.

The messenger continued, "The trumpets, sackbuts, psalteries, fifes, tabors, and cymbals and the shouting Romans make the Sun dance. Listen!"

The crowd of people shouted loudly.

"This is good news," Menenius said. "I will go and meet the ladies. This Volumnia is worth a city full of Consuls, Senators, and patricians. She is worth a sea and land full of Tribunes such as you. You have prayed well today. This morning I'd not have given a small coin for ten thousand of your throats."

The music and the shouting continued.

Sicinius said to the second messenger, "First, may the gods bless you for your tidings; next, accept my thankfulness."

The second messenger replied, "Sir, we all have great cause to give great thanks."

"Are the ladies near the city?" Sicinius asked.

"They are almost at the gates," the second messenger replied.

"We will meet them and join in the joy."

— 5.5 —

Two Senators escorted Volumnia, Virgilia, and Valeria on a street near the gate of Rome. Many other people were present.

The first Senator shouted, "Behold our patroness, the life of Rome! Call all your tribes together, praise the gods, and make triumphant fires; strew flowers before the ladies. Unshout the noise that banished Martius, and recall him to Rome with the welcome of his mother. All cry, 'Welcome, ladies, welcome!'"

All cried, "Welcome, ladies, welcome!"

Tullus Aufidius and some attendants were in a public place in the Volscian city of Antium.

Aufidius said, "Go and tell the lords of the city that I am here. Deliver this paper to them. After they have read it, tell them to go to the marketplace, where I in their hearing and in the hearing of the commoners will vouch for the truth of what I have written. Martius, whom I accuse, by this time has entered the city gates and intends to appear before the people, hoping to establish his innocence with words. Hurry and complete your task."

He gave the paper to an attendant, who exited along with the other attendants.

Some people who were conspiring with Aufidius against Coriolanus arrived.

Aufidius greeted them, "You are very welcome here!"

The first conspirator asked, "How is it with our General?"

Was he referring to Aufidius, or to Coriolanus?

Aufidius replied, "Just as it is with a man who has been poisoned by his own alms and slain as a result of his own charity."

Aufidius' alms had been to treat Coriolanus well when he first arrived in Antium as an exile; Coriolanus' alms had been to make a peace treaty with Rome. Either man could end up slain on this day. The common people of Antium would refer to Coriolanus as their General, but Aufidius' co-conspirators could very well refer to Aufidius as their General.

"Most noble sir," the second conspirator said, "if you still have the same intent wherein you wished us to be your accessories, we'll deliver you from your great danger."

"Sir, I cannot tell right now what I will do," Aufidius said. "We must proceed according to what we find out about the common people. We will find out how the common people feel, and we will proceed accordingly."

The third conspirator said, "The common people will remain uncertain while there's rivalry between you and Martius, but the fall of either of you will make the survivor the heir and winner of all."

"I know it," Aufidius said, "and my pretext to strike at him can be interpreted favorably. I raised Martius to a high position in our society, and I pawned my honor for his loyalty. Being so heightened and raised to a position of power, he watered his new plants — those men on whom he conferred honors — with dews of flattery, thereby seducing my friends. To achieve this end, he bowed his nature, which was never before known to be other than rough, unswayable, frank, and uncontrollable."

The third conspirator said, "Sir, his obstinacy when he ran to be elected Consul, which he lost by lack of stooping and lack of showing humility —"

"I was going to mention that," Aufidius said. "Being banished because of his lack of humility, he came to my hearth and presented his throat to my knife. I took him in, made him my equal partner in serving the Volscian state, and gave way to him in all his own desires. Indeed, I let him choose my best and freshest men from out of my files of soldiers, so he could accomplish his projects. I served his undertakings in my own person. I helped to reap the fame that he harvested as only his own. I took some pride in doing myself this wrong, until, at the end, I seemed to be his follower and not his partner, and he patronized me with a look of approval as if I had been no more than a mercenary — a hired soldier."

"So he did, my lord," the first conspirator said. "The army marveled at it, and, at the end, when he had conquered Rome and we looked for spoil no less than we looked for glory —"

"That was the thing for which my muscles shall be strained to the utmost against him," Aufidius said. "For a few drops of women's tears, which are as cheap as lies, he sold the blood and labor of our great military action; therefore, he shall die, and in his fall I'll regain my old position of honor. But, listen!"

Drums and trumpets sounded, and the common people shouted as they escorted Coriolanus.

The first conspirator said to Aufidius, "Your native town you entered like a messenger, and you were given no welcomes home, but now when he returns, the air is split with noise."

The second conspirator said, "And long-suffering fools, whose children he has slain, tear their base throats by shouting and giving him glory."

The third conspirator said, "Therefore, while you have your opportunity, before he expresses himself and moves the common people with his words, let him feel your sword. We will back you up with our swords. When he lies prostrate, dead, you can tell his story in a way that favors you, and we shall bury his explanations with his body."

"Say no more," Aufidius said. "Here come the lords."

The lords of the city walked over to Aufidius and his fellow conspirators.

"You are very welcome home," the lords said to Aufidius.

"I have not deserved it," Aufidius said. "But, worthy lords, have you carefully read the paper I wrote?"

"We have," the lords said.

"And we grieve to read it," the first lord said. "What faults he made before the most recent fault, I think might have been given light, easy-to-bear punishment. But he ended the war where things stood at the war's beginning; he gave away the benefit of our levies of soldiers.

"He answers us with our own charge: He returns to us only money for the expenses we laid out for the war, and he says that he acted under the authority we gave him.

"We should have conquered Rome and made great profit, but we get only a peace treaty, which we had before the war started, although Rome had yielded to our soldiers — this admits no excuse."

"He is approaching," Aufidius said. "You shall hear what he has to say."

Coriolanus arrived, marching with a drum and flying colors; the common people accompanied him.

"Hail, lords!" Coriolanus said. "I have returned as your soldier. I am no more infected with my country's love than when I departed from here, and I still remain under your great command. You need to know that my endeavors on your behalf have been prosperous; with bloody passage I led your wars even to the gates of Rome. Our spoils we have brought home more than counterpoise a full and a third part the expenses of the military action: The spoils amount to the cost of the war plus one third more. We have made peace with no less honor to the Antiates than shame to the Romans, and we here deliver, subscribed by the Roman Consuls and patricians, together with the seal of the Roman Senate, the peace terms we have settled on."

He offered the lords a scroll.

"Don't read it, noble lords," Aufidius said, "but tell the traitor that in the highest degree he has abused the powers you gave him."

"'Traitor'!" Coriolanus said. "What are you saying?"

"Yes! Traitor, Martius!" Aufidius said, not using the honorary title "Coriolanus."

"'Martius'!" Coriolanus said.

"Yes, Martius, Caius Martius," Aufidius said. "Do you think I'll honor you with that robbery — the name 'Coriolanus' you stole in Corioli?

"You lords and heads of the state, he has perfidiously betrayed your business, and given up, for certain drops of salty tears, Rome — which I say is your city — to his wife and mother. He has broken his oath and resolution as if they were a thread of rotten silk, never counseling other officers of the war, but at his nurse's — his mother's — tears he whined and howled away your victory, with the result that pages blushed because they were embarrassed for him and men of courage looked wondering at each other in astonishment."

"Do you hear this, Mars, god of war!" Coriolanus said.

"Don't name that god, you boy of tears, any more!" Aufidius said.

Coriolanus snorted and said, "Infinite liar, you have made my heart swell and grow too big for my chest. You call me 'boy'! You slave!

"Pardon me, lords, it is the first time that I was ever forced to scold and use violent language."

Coriolanus may have meant that it was the first time he did this in this city.

He continued, "Your judgments, my grave lords, must accuse this cur — this dog — of lying. His own understanding — the understanding of a man who wears striped scars made by my sword upon his body, stripes that he will bear to his grave — shall also show that he is lying."

The first lord said, "Both of you, be quiet, and hear me speak."

Angry, Coriolanus said, "Cut me to pieces, Volscians; men and lads, stain — discolor and dishonor — the edges of all your swords with my blood.

"'Boy'! You false hound!

"If you Volscians have written your histories correctly, you can read in them that, like an eagle in a dove-cote, I fluttered your Volscians in Corioli.

"Alone I did it. 'Boy'!"

Aufidius said, "Why, noble lords, will you be reminded of his blind luck, which was your shame, by this unholy braggart, before your own eyes and ears?"

All the conspirators shouted, "Let him die for it!"

The common people began to shout:

"Tear him to pieces!"

"Do it immediately!"

"He killed my son."

"He killed my daughter."

"He killed my cousin Marcus."

"He killed my father."

The second lord shouted, "Peace! Be quiet! Let there be no outrage! Peace!

"The man is noble and his fame is spread across the earth. His recent offences against us shall have a judicious and judicial hearing.

"Stand back, Aufidius, and do not trouble the peace."

Coriolanus said, "Oh, I wish that I had him, with six Aufidiuses, or better, his entire tribe of relatives, in a place where I could use my sword lawfully!"

"Insolent villain!" Aufidius shouted.

The conspirators shouted, "Kill him! Kill him! Kill him! Kill him! Kill him!"

The conspirators drew their swords and killed Coriolanus.

Aufidius stood on Coriolanus' body.

The lords cried, "Stop, stop, stop, stop!"

"My noble masters, hear me speak," Aufidius said.

The first lord said, "Oh, Tullus —"

The second lord said, "You have done a deed that will make valor weep."

"Don't tread on him," the third lord said. "Masters, be quiet; sheathe your swords."

Aufidius said, "My lords, when you shall know — as in this rage, which was provoked by him, you cannot — the great danger that this man's life put you in, you'll rejoice that he is dead. If it pleases your honors to call me before your Senate, I'll show that I am your loyal servant, or else I will endure your heaviest punishment."

The first lord said, "Bear away from here Coriolanus' body, and mourn for him. Let him be regarded as the most noble corpse that a herald ever followed to his tomb."

In this society, a herald would follow the corpse of an important person in a funeral and declaim the dead man's titles and accomplishments.

The second lord said, "Coriolanus' own anger takes away from Aufidius a great part of the blame. Let's make the best of it."

"My rage is gone," Aufidius said, "and I am struck with sorrow. Take his corpse up. Help, three of the chiefest soldiers; I'll be one of the people carrying the corpse. Beat the drum so that it sounds mournfully. Let your steel pikes trail on the ground. Though in this city he widowed and made childless many people who to this hour bewail the injury, yet he shall have a noble memorial and be nobly remembered. Assist me."

They lifted the corpse and carried it away, accompanied by all. A dead march — solemn music played at a funeral —sounded as they walked away.

APPENDIX A: ABOUT THE AUTHOR

It was a dark and stormy night. Suddenly a cry rang out, and on a hot summer night in 1954, Josephine, wife of Carl Bruce, gave birth to a boy — me. Unfortunately, this young married couple allowed Reuben Saturday, Josephine's brother, to name their first-born. Reuben, aka "The Joker," decided that Bruce was a nice name, so he decided to name me Bruce Bruce. I have gone by my middle name — David — ever since.

Being named Bruce David Bruce hasn't been all bad. Bank tellers remember me very quickly, so I don't often have to show an ID. It can be fun in charades, also. When I was a counselor as a teenager at Camp Echoing Hills in Warsaw, Ohio, a fellow counselor gave the signs for "sounds like" and "two words," then she pointed to a bruise on her leg twice. Bruise Bruise? Oh yeah, Bruce Bruce is the answer!

Uncle Reuben, by the way, gave me a haircut when I was in kindergarten. He cut my hair short and shaved a small bald spot on the back of my head. My mother wouldn't let me go to school until the bald spot grew out again.

Of all my brothers and sisters (six in all), I am the only transplant to Athens, Ohio. I was born in Newark, Ohio, and have lived all around Southeastern Ohio. However, I moved to Athens to go to Ohio University and have never left.

At Ohio U, I never could make up my mind whether to major in English or Philosophy, so I got a bachelor's degree with a double major in both areas, then I added a master's degree in English and a master's degree in Philosophy. Yes, I have my MAMA degree.

Currently, and for a long time to come (I eat fruits and veggies), I am spending my retirement writing books such as *Nadia Comaneci: Perfect 10*, *The Funniest People in Dance*, *Homer's* Iliad: *A Retelling in Prose*, and *William Shakespeare's* Othello: *A Retelling in Prose*.

By the way, my sister Brenda Kennedy writes romances such as *A New Beginning* and *Shattered Dreams*.

APPENDIX B: SOME BOOKS BY DAVID BRUCE

Retellings of a Classic Work of Literature

Arden of Faversham*: A Retelling*

Ben Jonson's The Alchemist: *A Retelling*

Ben Jonson's The Arraignment, or Poetaster: *A Retelling*

Ben Jonson's Bartholomew Fair: *A Retelling*

Ben Jonson's The Case is Altered: *A Retelling*

Ben Jonson's Catiline's Conspiracy: *A Retelling*

Ben Jonson's The Devil is an Ass: *A Retelling*

Ben Jonson's Epicene: *A Retelling*

Ben Jonson's Every Man in His Humor: *A Retelling*

Ben Jonson's Every Man Out of His Humor: *A Retelling*

Ben Jonson's The Fountain of Self-Love, or Cynthia's Revels: *A Retelling*

Ben Jonson's The Magnetic Lady, or Humors Reconciled: *A Retelling*

Ben Jonson's The New Inn, or The Light Heart: *A Retelling*

Ben Jonson's Sejanus' Fall: *A Retelling*

Ben Jonson's The Staple of News: *A Retelling*

Ben Jonson's A Tale of a Tub: *A Retelling*

Ben Jonson's Volpone, or the Fox: *A Retelling*

Christopher Marlowe's Complete Plays: Retellings

Christopher Marlowe's Dido, Queen of Carthage: *A Retelling*

Christopher Marlowe's Doctor Faustus: *Retellings of the 1604 A-Text and of the 1616 B-Text*

Christopher Marlowe's Edward II: *A Retelling*

Christopher Marlowe's The Massacre at Paris: *A Retelling*

Christopher Marlowe's The Rich Jew of Malta: *A Retelling*

Christopher Marlowe's Tamburlaine, Parts 1 and 2: *Retellings*

Dante's Divine Comedy: *A Retelling in Prose*

Dante's Inferno: *A Retelling in Prose*

Dante's Purgatory: *A Retelling in Prose*

Dante's Paradise: *A Retelling in Prose*

The Famous Victories of Henry V: *A Retelling*

From the Iliad *to the* Odyssey: *A Retelling in Prose of Quintus of Smyrna's* Posthomerica

George Chapman, Ben Jonson, and John Marston's Eastward Ho! *A Retelling*

George Peele's The Arraignment of Paris: *A Retelling*

George Peele's The Battle of Alcazar: *A Retelling*

George Peele's David and Bathsheba, and the Tragedy of Absalom: *A Retelling*

George Peele's Edward I: *A Retelling*

George Peele's The Old Wives' Tale: *A Retelling*

George-a-Greene: *A Retelling*

The History of King Leir: *A Retelling*

Homer's Iliad: *A Retelling in Prose*

Homer's Odyssey: *A Retelling in Prose*

J.W. Gent.'s The Valiant Scot: *A Retelling*

Jason and the Argonauts: A Retelling in Prose of Apollonius of Rhodes' Argonautica

John Ford: Eight Plays Translated into Modern English

John Ford's The Broken Heart: *A Retelling*

John Ford's The Fancies, Chaste and Noble: *A Retelling*

John Ford's The Lady's Trial: *A Retelling*

John Ford's The Lover's Melancholy: *A Retelling*

John Ford's Love's Sacrifice: *A Retelling*

John Ford's Perkin Warbeck: *A Retelling*

John Ford's The Queen: *A Retelling*

John Ford's 'Tis Pity She's a Whore: *A Retelling*

John Lyly's Campaspe: *A Retelling*

John Lyly's Endymion, The Man in the Moon: *A Retelling*

John Lyly's Galatea: *A Retelling*

John Lyly's Love's Metamorphosis: *A Retelling*

John Lyly's Midas: *A Retelling*

John Lyly's Mother Bombie: *A Retelling*

John Lyly's Sappho and Phao: *A Retelling*

John Lyly's The Woman in the Moon: *A Retelling*

John Webster's The White Devil: *A Retelling*

King Edward III: *A Retelling*

Mankind: *A Medieval Morality Play* (A Retelling)

Margaret Cavendish's The Unnatural Tragedy: *A Retelling*

The Merry Devil of Edmonton: *A Retelling*

The Summoning of Everyman: *A Medieval Morality Play* (A Retelling)

Robert Greene's Friar Bacon and Friar Bungay: *A Retelling*

The Taming of a Shrew: *A Retelling*

Tarlton's Jests: A Retelling

Thomas Middleton's A Chaste Maid in Cheapside: *A Retelling*

Thomas Middleton's Women Beware Women: *A Retelling*

Thomas Middleton and Thomas Dekker's The Roaring Girl: *A Retelling*

Thomas Middleton and William Rowley's The Changeling: *A Retelling*

The Trojan War and Its Aftermath: Four Ancient Epic Poems

Virgil's Aeneid: *A Retelling in Prose*

William Shakespeare's 5 Late Romances: Retellings in Prose

William Shakespeare's 10 Histories: Retellings in Prose

William Shakespeare's 11 Tragedies: Retellings in Prose

William Shakespeare's 12 Comedies: Retellings in Prose

William Shakespeare's 38 Plays: Retellings in Prose

William Shakespeare's 1 Henry IV, aka Henry IV, Part 1: *A Retelling in Prose*

William Shakespeare's 2 Henry IV, aka Henry IV, Part 2: *A Retelling in Prose*

William Shakespeare's 1 Henry VI, aka Henry VI, Part 1: *A Retelling in Prose*

William Shakespeare's 2 Henry VI, aka Henry VI, Part 2: *A Retelling in Prose*

William Shakespeare's 3 Henry VI, aka Henry VI, Part 3: *A Retelling in Prose*

William Shakespeare's All's Well that Ends Well: *A Retelling in Prose*

William Shakespeare's Antony and Cleopatra: *A Retelling in Prose*

William Shakespeare's As You Like It: *A Retelling in Prose*

William Shakespeare's The Comedy of Errors: *A Retelling in Prose*

William Shakespeare's Coriolanus: *A Retelling in Prose*

William Shakespeare's Cymbeline: *A Retelling in Prose*

William Shakespeare's Hamlet: *A Retelling in Prose*

William Shakespeare's Henry V: *A Retelling in Prose*

William Shakespeare's Henry VIII: *A Retelling in Prose*

William Shakespeare's Julius Caesar: *A Retelling in Prose*

William Shakespeare's King John: *A Retelling in Prose*

William Shakespeare's King Lear: *A Retelling in Prose*

William Shakespeare's Love's Labor's Lost: *A Retelling in Prose*

William Shakespeare's Macbeth: *A Retelling in Prose*

William Shakespeare's Measure for Measure: *A Retelling in Prose*

William Shakespeare's The Merchant of Venice: *A Retelling in Prose*

William Shakespeare's The Merry Wives of Windsor: *A Retelling in Prose*

William Shakespeare's A Midsummer Night's Dream: *A Retelling in Prose*

William Shakespeare's Much Ado About Nothing: *A Retelling in Prose*

William Shakespeare's Othello: *A Retelling in Prose*

William Shakespeare's Pericles, Prince of Tyre: *A Retelling in Prose*

William Shakespeare's Richard II: *A Retelling in Prose*

William Shakespeare's Richard III: *A Retelling in Prose*

William Shakespeare's Romeo and Juliet: *A Retelling in Prose*

William Shakespeare's The Taming of the Shrew: *A Retelling in Prose*

William Shakespeare's The Tempest: *A Retelling in Prose*

William Shakespeare's Timon of Athens: *A Retelling in Prose*

William Shakespeare's Titus Andronicus: *A Retelling in Prose*

William Shakespeare's Troilus and Cressida: *A Retelling in Prose*

William Shakespeare's Twelfth Night: *A Retelling in Prose*

William Shakespeare's The Two Gentlemen of Verona: *A Retelling in Prose*

William Shakespeare's The Two Noble Kinsmen: *A Retelling in Prose*

William Shakespeare's The Winter's Tale: *A Retelling in Prose*